# RAVEN III

## Balm of Gilead

D.M. BARRETT

Published in 2020 by Amazon Printing.

Cover design by: Mat Yan Cover Designs

Library of Congress Cataloguing

ISBN:  979-8-619-04007-4
Printed in the United States of America

# DEDICATION

This book is dedicated to my lovely wife, Marilyn, and my beautiful daughter, Jennifer. Without their diligence in proofing, editing and thoughtful suggestions, this finished work would not have been possible.

# TABLE OF CONTENTS

# 1. The Peddler

After concluding their honeymoon and attending to the passing of Boyd Miller, the preacher and the county nurse returned to Ferguson. They took temporary residence at Miss Rosie's. Things went smoothly for the first week, but by the second week their stay started hitting a few bumps.

Nurse Bilbrey, now Nurse Bilbrey-Mann, made her way to the end of the long hallway to the stairs that led to the main parlor. Miss Rosie was waiting for her with a stern look on her face.

"Miss Rosie, I've never seen you with a frown," the county nurse remarked.

"It happens but it's not often," she replied.

"What's the problem?" Nurse Mann asked.

"I hate to bring it up, but your husband is disturbing my other guests," Miss Rosie replied.

"What has he done?" the nurse asked with surprise.

"Just give it a couple of minutes and you'll find out," Miss Rosie instructed.

From the end of the hallway came the sound of a band that seemed almost identical to the Smith

Brothers. It wasn't long before the preacher began to croon the tune "Somebody Touched Me:"

"While I was preaching somebody touched me,
While I was preaching somebody touched me,
While I was preaching somebody touched me,
It must've been the hand of the Lord.
Glory, glory, glory, somebody touched me,
Glory, glory, glory, somebody touched me,
Glory, glory, glory, somebody touched me,
It must've been the hand of the Lord."

Miss Rosie motioned for Nurse Mann to follow her down the staircase to the large parlor. She wasn't finished with this discussion

"Now don't get me wrong, that preacher can sing well. In fact, I've heard him several times on the Friday Night Frolics. He always gets loud applause. He even gets fan mail occasionally," Miss Rosie explained.

"Are the guests' complaints against his singing?" the county nurse inquired.

"It's the timing of his singing. Most folks come here to relax, sleep late, have a late breakfast, and cast off their worries. The moment you leave to make your rounds the preacher starts his concert. It's only 7:00 am and he is in full revival mode!" Miss Rosie lamented.

"How many songs does he usually sing?" Nurse Mann asked.

"He always sings three. He never sings more, and he never sings less." Miss Rosie replied.

"That is because Jeremy Ford sent off for a new Victrola machine for Tom. He used the record cutting machine he made to produce three Smith Brothers tunes for WNOX-AM for airplay on one side and instrumentals only on the back side for advertising backgrounds," Nurse Mann explained.

"How did the preacher get them?" Miss Rosie inquired.

"Jeremy and Tom are the very best of friends after they came up with that portable water heater. He made an extra set of records for the preacher," Nurse Mann reported.

"I've had guests tell me he's better at waking them up than an old Leghorn rooster at sunrise!" Miss Rosie exclaimed.

"I'll talk to him. Finis Martin's men should have our house finished within another month. When we move in, he'll only have to keep the volume down to keep from waking up Little Man and upsetting SheMammy," Nurse Mann said with a chuckle.

"Don't you dare tell him you heard anything from me. I wouldn't hurt that man's feelings for $10,000," Miss Rosie announced.

"Don't worry. I'll tell him he's singing far too early for your guests. Besides, the other day he told me I needed some blush on my cheeks because I looked like a haint," the county nurse said.

"I'm surprised he can still sing after that comment," Miss Rosie said with a laugh.

"We're both still in marriage training," the county nurse said, as she smiled and headed toward the front door.

\*      \*      \*

At about 11:30 am Preacher Mann walked through the front door of Discount Grocery. Jack Wright was speaking to his new peddling truck driver who finished half of his Wednesday peddling route.

"How are sales, Hans?" the preacher asked.

"They are brisk, but a few customers would not buy anything from me today," Hans Shultz replied.

"Because of what's happening in Europe, a few families are not pleased with anyone of German descent," Jack Wright remarked.

"I understand their ire. I am not happy with things that are happening in Europe either," the peddler remarked with a shrug.

"I'm afraid things will get worse. The United States is a declared neutral, but we are sending every type of equipment, supplies, and food possible to England under the Lend-Lease Act," Preacher Mann predicted.

4

"Do you think the United States will enter the war?" Jack Wright inquired.

"Only with the entry of the United States into the war will the Nazis be stopped," Hans Shultz said sadly.

"That's a hard sell here, Hans. We think one World War in 20 years in Europe is enough. Unless attacked directly, we'll most likely sit this one out," Preacher Mann replied.

"I had spoken enough of political matters today. I will now return to my peddling route to make money for Mr. Wright," Hans said as he walked toward the rear door of Discount Grocery.

"Are you losing sales because of him?" Preacher Mann inquired.

"Yes. I need to find a way to calm the fears of the few distrustful families," Jack Wright said.

"Gary Simpkins has recently transferred from the ATU to the FBI. I'll get our old friend, Whitehorse, to get Hans Schultz a clear record. If asked, he'll likely send a letter to you as his employer," Preacher Mann suggested.

"That'd be great. It's just what we need," Jack Wright said.

"I'll call him now," the preacher replied.

\* \* \*

5

The preacher made his usual Friday lunch stop at the Bluebird Café. He was able to enjoy a midday meal and hear the Smith Brothers practice for their Friday Night Frolics broadcast.

"Preacher, we've got a country ham platter and a fried chicken platter as specials today," Doris Smith said with a smile.

"Doris, this brings to mind an Old Testament Bible verse," Preacher Mann said with a slight chuckle.

"Give me today's sermonette, preacher," Doris said with a huge smile.

"Multitudes, multitudes in the valley of decision," he replied.

"Now preacher, we both know you made up your mind in less than a minute. It's gonna be the country ham platter," Doris remarked.

Before the preacher could reply, a male voice said, "Make that three."

When the preacher looked up, it was Special Agent Gary Simpkins and Special Agent John Jenkins. Whitehorse extended his hand as did Agent Jenkins. After two hearty handshakes, the preacher invited them to be seated.

"I guess chasing 'shiners at the ATU got too boring and you decided to chase bank robbers, gangsters, and spies," Preacher Mann remarked.

The FBI agents looked at each other but did not respond. The preacher sensed uneasiness, but he was not overly concerned.

"Did you take Revenue Agent Rogers with you?" Preacher Mann asked.

"Actually, he took my old job as chief," Whitehorse replied.

The three men were interrupted by Cecil Smith. The preacher knew he always got to make the first song request at the Friday practice session.

"What's your request today?" Cecil Smith asked.

"I want to hear 'Rabbit in The Log,'" the preacher replied.

Hearing the preacher's request, the Smith Brothers' Band began the song's instrumental introduction as Cecil Smith grabbed the microphone and began to sing:

**"There's a rabbit in the log and I ain't got no dog**
**How will I get him I know (I know)**
**I'll get me a briar and I'll twist it in his hair**
**That's how I'll get him I know."**

After a few songs the Smith Brothers took a break and Agent Simpkins, Agent Jenkins, and Preacher Mann were almost finished with their meal. Doris cleared the dishes and the three men waited for their apple cobbler desert.

"Raven, do you know something about Hans Shultz you're not sharing with us?" Whitehorse asked.

"What gives you that idea?" the preacher queried.

"First you make a remark about us chasing spies. Then, you choose a song about getting a rabbit out of a log," Gary Simpkins replied.

"I failed to see the connection," the preacher said with a puzzled look.

"What I'm about to tell you is strictly confidential. I know you'll keep it that way or we wouldn't share it with you," Agent Simpkins said.

"Say on," Preacher Mann said.

Whitehorse nodded to Agent Jenkins who began, "One of the principal reasons we are working out of the FBI office in Knoxville is we are tasked with investigating subversives, spies, acts of espionage, and other threats to national security."

"I can see why you were rattled by my characterizing your new positions as chasing spies," the preacher replied.

"The man you asked us to check out is not Hans Shultz. His real name is Hans Gruber. He's a former German SS Captain. He's a deserter. We made a few calls to military intelligence and bells and whistles went off," Agent Simpkins explained.

8

"What's worse is the code name given to him by military intelligence is 'the rabbit,'" Agent Jenkins remarked.

"I suppose you are dealing with a rabbit in the log," Preacher Mann said with a sigh.

"The next piece of information is highly classified. We have clearance to share it but it's for your ears only," Whitehorse said.

"I'm listening," Preacher Mann said.

"There's a top-secret research facility being built near Knoxville. There is considerable worry that Hans Gruber is truly a spy to keep tabs on the facility," Gary Simpkins explained.

"What can you tell us about him?" Agent Jenkins inquired.

"He's not a fan of the Nazis or what is happening in Europe. He's running a peddling truck for Discount Grocery. Apart from a few families who don't care for Germans, he's well liked and does a good job," the preacher reported.

"What's your opinion?" Gary Simpson queried.

"You guys are the experts. Why are you asking me?" Preacher Mann asked with a puzzled look.

"You know every heartbeat of every person in this town. Who would know better about a man's attitude, actions, intentions, etc. than you?" Agent Simpkins asked.

"I have no suspicions of Hans Shultz or Hans Gruber. I trust him. I do have some angst about his proximity to a top-secret research facility," Preacher Mann remarked.

"How well do you know him?" Agent Simpkins inquired.

"He's been here close to a year. I am not aware of any problems. His family attends Community Church. I mostly exchanged pleasantries with him and his family," the preacher explained.

The two special agents looked at each other and then at the preacher. Agent Simpkins nodded to Agent Jenkins to speak.

"Hans Gruber was the officer in charge of a top-secret German research facility similar to the one we told you about. His job was mostly security. He was not a scientist., but he could have valuable information that could help us in many ways," Agent Jenkins said.

"How does this involve me?" Preacher Mann asked.

"We want you to get him to talk to us. He knows you. He trusts you. We could take him into custody but think it would be counter-productive at this point," Whitehorse said.

"Will he be detained? Will he be forcibly relocated?" the preacher asked.

"That depends," Agent Jenkins replied.

"It depends on what?" Preacher Mann asked.

"It depends on how the meeting and interview turn out, but we'd like to keep him in Ferguson. We could keep tabs on him and use his knowledge to help our efforts," Gary Simpkins explained.

"Meet me at Miss Rosie's at 3:30 pm. He gets back to Discount Grocery and unpacks the peddling truck until his Monday peddling run. I'll have Jack Wright tell him I need to speak with him," Preacher Mann instructed.

"We'll give you time to speak with him before you make the introduction. After you've had about ten minutes with him, we'll appear at the table," Agent Jenkins said.

"If I'm doing government work today, you can pay the bill. Be sure to leave a generous tip," Preacher Mann said, as he stood and pointed for Doris Smith to give the lunch ticket to Agent Gary Simpkins.

*    *    *

At almost 4:00 pm, the German peddler entered Miss Rosie's dining room and made his way to Preacher Mann's table. He was smiling as the preacher motioned for him to sit down.

"Mr. Wright said you wanted to speak to me but warned me you did not care for gossip unless it involved him," Hans said with a large smile.

11

"Actually, I have two long-term friends I want you to meet. I think you will be able to help them, and they will help you. I know these men and I am convinced that what they can offer will greatly benefit you and your family," Preacher Mann said.

"Based upon your confidence in the men, I will gladly speak to them," Hans Shultz said.

Preacher Mann motioned for the two men to approach the table. He introduced them as his friends.

"Hans, I asked these men to gather some information we could use to eliminate any fear the citizens of this area may harbor about a German. When they checked with other American authorities, it came to our attention you are wanted by Germany for desertion, among other things. That is not their concern, but your former line of work is of interest," Preacher Mann explained.

"This is true. I will answer any questions truthfully about my life and work," the peddler replied.

"I will be at another table while you three men talk. If you have concerns or need to ask something, let me know and I will return. However, your former life is not my business. Their interest in your work is not my business either," the preacher instructed.

Agents Simpkins and Jenkins interviewed Hans Gruber, now Hans Shultz, for about two hours. Agent

Simpkins asked most of the questions and Agent Jenkins took notes.

When the interview was concluded, Agent Simpkins motioned for the preacher to join them at the table. Since the three men were smiling, the preacher surmised things had gone well.

"Here's the situation. Hans Shultz has been a tremendous help to us. We will have several future visits with him. We have a mutual understanding that he and his family will remain in Putnam County and continue his peddling route. If he experiences any difficulties or needs to go outside the county, he must notify one of us," Gary Simpkins explained.

"Is there any chance we can get some sort of document or letter that suggests he is not a threat to the citizens of this area?" Preacher Mann inquired.

"That is above our pay grade but it's likely. You can vouch for him in the interim," Agent Jenkins said.

"Hans, you are excused. We want to visit with the preacher before we return to Knoxville tonight," Agent Simpkins explained.

Hans shook hands with the two agents and whispered to Preacher Mann, "Thank you'" before heading for the door.

"Raven, you've got another preacher in Ferguson now. Why don't you come to Knoxville and work for the Bureau? We need men like you. You get things done," Whitehorse implored.

"I am doing a great work, so that I cannot come down. Why should the work cease while I leave it and go down to you?" the preacher said quoting from Nehemiah 6:3.

"What does that mean?" Agent John Jenkins asked.

"It his polite way of telling us what he's doing is more important than what we're asking him to do," Agent Simpkins explained.

The two agents stood and exchanged handshakes. The preacher bade them a fond farewell.

"If the situation turns into a shooting war, Raven may have no choice but to change occupations for a while," Whitehorse remarked.

"Indeed," Agent Jenkins remarked as the two men exited Miss Rosie's.

## 2. Whisperers

Preacher Mann and his beautiful wife awoke to the sound of a light rapping on the door of their room at Miss Rosie's. Since it was slightly before 7:00 am on a Monday, they were surprised anyone would be calling at that hour.

"Are you going to answer the door?" the preacher inquired.

"I'm naked," Nurse Mann exclaimed in a voice slightly above a whisper.

"Who is it?" Preacher Mann inquired.

"It's Rosie Hatton. Come to the door. I need to talk to you," she replied.

"I'm like Adam in the Garden of Eden," the preacher replied.

"How's that?" Miss Rosie queried.

"I heard thy voice . . . and I was afraid, because I was naked; and I hid myself," the preacher quoted.

"Well, you ain't got nothin' I ain't seen before. But crack the door and stand behind it. I need to tell you something," Miss Rosie instructed.

The preacher did as Miss Rosie requested. His wife stood beside him, behind the slightly opened door.

15

"What's got you knocking on my door so early, Miss Rosie?" the preacher asked.

"SheMammy Martin stopped by on his way to take Little Man for his monthly check-up at Dr. Whitman's. He's going to leave him with Anna Mae so he can be back in 30 minutes to speak with you and your wife. He said it's important," Miss Rosie explained.

"It may take a little longer than a half-hour for us to get ready," the preacher speculated.

"Do a double-up. You'll save some time," Miss Rosie suggested.

"What's a double-up?" the county nurse asked.

"Get in that shower together without any hanky-panky," Miss Rosie instructed.

"I like your way of thinking," Nurse Mann said.

"Preacher, here's a verse for you: 'Flee also youthful lusts,'" Miss Rosie said.

"I'm not youthful," the preacher replied.

"Then you shouldn't have a problem getting ready in half an hour," Miss Rosie said curtly as she started down the hall.

The county nurse nodded her head and moved toward the bathroom. The preacher followed.

Promptly at 7:30 am the couple descended the large staircase leading from the top level of Miss Rosie's to the main parlor. They turned to their left and entered the large dining room. Clayton Martin was having coffee and a pastry. He stood up until Nurse Mann could be seated.

"How's Little Man?" the county nurse inquired.

"He's doing great. Dr. Whitman is monitoring his hips monthly to make sure they stay in the proper positions. No problems in the last six months," Mr. Martin reported.

"That's great," the preacher said.

"Preacher, do you remember the first rule of SheMammy?" Clayton Martin inquired.

"What happens with SheMammy stays with SheMammy. It is a vow of confidentiality for your customers," Preacher Mann responded.

"When someone talks confidentially to their preacher, what's the most important thing?" Clayton Martin queried.

"It's not any different. Things are kept confidential. It's legally referred to as the clergy-penitent privilege," Preacher Mann replied.

"Well, this is the first time in my life I'm going to break the first rule of SheMammy. You have my permission to use the information exchange as you see fit," Mr. Martin said.

"Do I need to leave?" Nurse Mann inquired.

"You've got the same confidentiality rule as does any medical provider. You can, and should, stay," Clayton Martin explained.

"What has you so upset as to bend SheMammy's most important rule?" the preacher asked.

"I think there's some serious hanky-panky going on with Josh Sullivan and Miss Patricia Stoner-Barrett, the schoolteacher," SheMammy opined.

"Oh my," the county nurse exclaimed.

"Say on," Preacher Mann encouraged.

"He's been spending a lot of time with her at the lake, atop Brotherton Mountain. There's a clear view of that picnic spot from my parlor," Mr. Martin said.

"Anything else?" the preacher inquired.

"Josh helped her pick out a fabric for a French-style two- piece swimsuit. When I finished it a week later, she modeled it for him," SheMammy disclosed.

"I'm still listening," Preacher Mann said stoically.

"I saw them having a picnic, one of several I might add, and she was wearing that same red two-piece, skimpy swimsuit. This week they stopped by and Josh helped her pick out some very sexy lingerie," Clayton Martin concluded.

"Tom, you need to get to the bottom of this. It has scandal written all over it," the county nurse remarked.

"A person is innocent until proven guilty," the preacher said.

"Not when it's a preacher! You should listen to your own sermons. 'Abstain from all appearance of evil," Nurse Mann retorted.

"I have to agree with your wife. You need to check into this and take the appropriate action," Clayton Martin said.

"What do you consider as appropriate action?" the preacher asked.

"It depends on what you find out. It could be anything from gentle encouragement to running him off for cavorting with a married woman. Whatever you do should be done discreetly. We don't need a scandal in Ferguson. That's why I'm breaking SheMammy's number one rule," Clayton Martin explained.

SheMammy noticed Miss Rosie a couple of tables away. He decided to say nothing else and leave matters to be handled by the preacher. He stood, shook hands with the preacher, and made his way to the door.

"What do you think?" the county nurse asked.

"I think it's time to order," Preacher Mann said as Miss Rosie walked to the table.

After placing their breakfast orders with Miss Rosie, she said, "I'm giving these orders to the cook and coming back. There's something serious I need to speak with you about."

"Now what do you think?" Nurse Mann asked.

"It's like that gospel song the Smith Brothers sing called 'Stormy Waters.'

"Stormy waters around me
And the tempest and fury may roll
But I have my dear Savior
How he helps me nobody can know
When it seems I'm forsaken
And my earthly friends misunderstand
Stormy waters surround me
But I'll hold to God's unchanging hand."

Before Nurse Mann could respond, Miss Rosie returned to their table. She seated herself and looked directly at Preacher Mann.

"Now preacher, I know you hate a gossiper. If this makes me guilty, the good Lord can deliver the stripes to my back," Miss Rosie said with a slight break in her voice.

"What is upsetting you Miss Rosie?" the preacher asked.

"I've been making weekly picnic lunches this month for Josh. I thought he was courting that young county nurse, Abby," Miss Rosie reported.

"I know they both seem to have an interest in each other. I'm not surprised," Nurse Mann replied.

"Well, last week I walked to the window when he left with the basket. He was in Louis Barrett's car and the schoolteacher was driving," Miss Rosie said.

"It could have been for Louis, Patricia, and Josh," the preacher suggested.

"It was food for two. It was the same for the previous three weeks," Miss Rosie explained.

"Oh, my goodness," Nurse Mann exclaimed.

"I'll keep this confidential and check into the situation," the preacher said.

"I'll get your order. I know you both have things to do today," Miss Rosie said as she stood and made her way toward the kitchen.

"I'm waiting to hear your thoughts after that last report," the county nurse chided.

"The scripture says charity, meaning the pure love of God, 'thinketh no evil,'" the preacher replied.

"Ok, what do you intend to do?" Nurse Mann asked bluntly.

"I intend to consult the town gossip. If there's more to the story than we've heard, he will know about it," Preacher Mann said.

"I knew your first stop would be Discount Grocery," Nurse Mann said knowingly.

Before the preacher could reply, Miss Rosie delivered the couple's breakfast. Nurse Mann finished her meal, kissed Preacher Man, and said, "You're going to have a long day today."

"Indeed," the preacher remarked with a huge sigh.

\*     \*     \*

RAVEN III                               D.M. BARRETT

When the preacher arrived at Discount Grocery, Jack Wright was by himself. He was feverishly stocking shelves with canned goods.

"What's the rush?" Preacher Mann inquired.

"I'm filling the shelves before Hans Shultz gets here and starts filling the peddling truck," Jack Wright replied.

"I didn't realize there was a competition," the preacher replied.

"It's that damn German efficiency. I can't even take a break when he's around," Jack Wright said with a chuckle.

"I need to speak with you about something important," Preacher Mann said.

"I know what it's about," Jack Wright said with his head slightly lowered.

"Really?" the preacher responded with a surprised look.

"Marcia Lewis stopped by the store to tell me she's moving to Oak Ridge to work in a new government factory. I slipped her a quart of shine as a gift. We didn't drink a drop. I know someone told you she was at the store, but nothing happened. I doubt she'll be in the area again," the merchant explained.

"That's an interesting story but it's not what I'm wanting to discuss," Preacher Mann said.

"You mean I confessed for nothing?" Jack Wright exclaimed.

"You just gossiped on yourself," the preacher replied.

"I thought that *was* a confession," the storekeeper opined.

"If nothing happened, it doesn't qualify as a confession," the preacher remarked.

"Now that we've got that resolved, what are you wanting to know?" the merchant queried.

"The Lord forgives you," Preacher Mann said.

"For what?" Jack Wright inquired.

"For gossiping," the preacher responded.

"I haven't been gossiping. I'm taking your warning about gossiping seriously," the storekeeper exclaimed.

"Well, I'm going to ask *you* some gossip and ask you what you know," the preacher responded.

"Is this like a test? You know, like Abraham being told to sacrifice Isaac?" Jack Wright queried.

"It's not a test. I need to know what you know about Josh Sullivan spending a lot of time with the schoolteacher," Preacher Mann said bluntly.

"It's true but I don't think there's any fire with that smoke," Jack Wright opined.

"Why do you hold that opinion?" the preacher inquired.

"Louis Barrett knows they've been having picnics at the lake together. In fact, I've heard him even suggest it. Josh has been working a lot at the newspaper, earning money and learning the printing business this summer," Jack Wright said.

"Anything else?" the preacher asked.

"Louis said Josh helped Patricia pick out a French-style swimsuit at SheMammy's place," Jack Wright said.

"Why in the world would he tell you that?" the preacher asked.

"I think he was happy she was stepping outside the traditional schoolteacher role. Also, I'm a reformed gossip. I just don't understand your concern. Louis and Patricia are just a few years older than Josh. They enjoy each other's company," Jack Wright responded.

"It revolves around the biblical concept of abstaining from the *appearance* of evil," Preacher Mann remarked.

"Taken to an extreme, one could become a slave to the perceptions or misperceptions of others. We'd spend all our time worrying about someone misconstruing our actions. Our goal is to live right before God. It is not to comply with others' arbitrary standards of conduct," Jack Wright opined.

"You might just be preaching that sermon next week. Unfortunately, most church members hold preachers to a higher standard. That's an important lesson for a young preacher to learn," Preacher Mann said.

"Well, you'll have to talk to the three of them. You shouldn't just single out Josh," Jack Wright remarked.

"Who are you going to be having a talk with, preacher?" Louis Barrett said as he entered Discount Grocery.

"Actually, I need to talk confidentially to you, your wife, and Josh," the preacher stated.

"Josh and Patricia and working on some print orders at the newspaper office right now. How about all of us meeting at Community Church at 3:00 pm this afternoon?" Louis Barrett suggested.

"I'll be there," Preacher Mann promised.

Louis Barrett nodded as he paid Jack Wright for the soft drink and peanuts he bought. Jack Wright and Preacher Mann gave surprised looks to each other.

\*    \*    \*

The preacher looked at his pocket watch. He noted it said 2:55 pm. As he placed the watch into his trouser watch pocket. The Barrett's and Josh Sullivan opened the door and walked into the church auditorium.

"I should have had this talk sooner, but I waited until my plans were more concrete," Josh Sullivan said.

"Say on," Preacher Mann replied.

"I've decided to transfer from my bachelor of divinity program at Vanderbilt to the secondary

education program at Middle Tennessee State
Teachers College. I can graduate by Christmas if I do
my teaching internship with Patricia at the Ferguson
school," Josh explained.

"Are you planning on leaving the ministry?" the
preacher asked.

"I'm not cut out to be a pulpit preacher or even to
do all the things you do," the young man lamented.

"I'm listening," Preacher Mann said.

"I want a life in religious education. With the help
of Louis and Patricia Barrett, we've figured out a way
to make it happen," Josh Sullivan explained.

"We propose a four-year Christian high school or
academy, conducted by correspondence to the
Tennessee Board of Education. If it is under the
auspices of Community Church with a duly
appointed board of trustees for the academy, it will be
unanimously approved," Patricia Barrett reported.

"Initially, Josh and Patricia can handle
corresponding with students, grading papers, etc. The
lesson manuals can be printed at The Mountain
Gazette. We can enlist you as board chairman and Joe
Scott, Dr. Whitman, me as trustees," Louis Barrett
suggested.

"What about the curriculum? What about the
costs?" Preacher Mann queried.

"The state requires a major area of study and one
minor area of study, four courses in English, one

course in math, one course in science, and one course each in American history and Tennessee history. A diploma can be awarded at the conclusion of 16 total courses," Josh Sullivan replied.

"We think within a couple of years the academy can be self-sustaining. It will depend on support from the church, interested donors, and a very small amount of tuition from each student annually," Louis Barrett added.

"Are the graduates eligible for entry into college?" the preacher asked.

"In Tennessee, it will be the same as any other high school. It will be up to other states based on their own set criteria. There will be disclaimers and explanations on the enrollment and application forms," Patricia Barrett said.

"What do you think? Do we have your support?" Josh asked with a look of supplication.

"I fully support the project. I will recommend it to the church after you give a full explanation to the congregation. But there is one condition that is binding on the three of you," Preacher Mann said sternly.

"What is that?" Josh Sullivan asked.

"The Community Church Minister of Education will not be picking out skimpy swimsuits for married women – even with their husband's approval. He will not be having picnics at the lake with married women.

He will follow the biblical admonition that is applicable to a preacher: Abstain from all *appearance* of evil. Church members hold preachers to a higher standard than everyone else. It goes with the job," Preacher Mann explained.

"Patricia and I take full responsibility. We both see Josh like a younger brother. But we'll heed your counsel," Louis Barrett explained.

"Is there anything else?" Patricia Barrett queried.

"Yes, get him married to Nurse Abby or some eligible young lady. I'm not ready to have any more birds and bees talks with him," Preacher Mann said with a chuckle.

"Anything else?" Josh Sullivan asked.

"What's the name of this school?" the preacher inquired.

"Tennessee Christian Academy," the three replied in unison.

# 3. Mountain Music & Art Festival

Preacher Mann removed his gold pocket watch from his watch pocket, looked at the time, and sighed loudly. The Ferguson Merchants Association was already ten minutes late starting, and none of the members were present except Miss Rosie.

"Preacher, patience is not just about waiting – it's about how we behave while we're waiting," Miss Rosie declared.

"What wise man said that?" the preacher inquired.

"My father, right before my fidgeting forced him to resort to sterner measures," Miss Rosie declared with her signature smile.

"Indeed," Preacher Mann replied.

"What do you think is causing their delay?" Nurse Mann asked.

"They're plotting something they want to get past the preacher," Miss Rosie said with a chuckle.

"Why are you meeting the other culprits?" Preacher Mann queried.

"Someone's got to keep you busy and fed till they show up,"
Miss Rosie remarked.

"So, you are in the middle of this conspiracy, too, Miss Rosie?" Nurse Mann asked.

"Honey, I'm the one who hatched it up," Miss Rosie responded.

"Confession is good for the soul, Miss Rosie," the preacher chided.

"We want you to be a judge at the Music and Art Festival," Miss Rosie admitted.

"I think the Smith Brothers would be better judges for the music contests and the Barrett's know more about art than I do," Preacher Mann said.

Before Miss Rosie could respond, Sheriff Hankins, Louis Barrett, Jack Wright, Cecil Smith, Miss Ruby, Martin Lawrence, and George Hickman entered the dining room at Miss Rosie's. They all walked toward the large dining table where Miss Rosie, the preacher, and the county nurse were sitting.

"Did you convince him, Miss Rosie?" Sheriff Hankins inquired.

"He didn't say no, but he didn't say yes," Miss Rosie replied.

"Preacher, it's your civic duty to the citizens of Ferguson to serve as its municipal judge during the festival and beyond," George Hickman said sternly.

"I thought she meant a judge for the music and art competition," the shocked preacher remarked.

"We've listed you for the judge on Friday in the clogging, gospel music, and paintings competitions," Jack Wright explained.

"Who came up with the need for a city judge, and who thought up this absurd idea that the local preacher should hold the job?" the preacher asked with incredulity.

"Sheriff Hankins thought it was time for a municipal judge. Miss Ruby nominated you. George Hickman seconded your nomination. The vote was unanimous," Louis Barrett explained.

"Is business so slack you feel the need to prosecute parking tickets, speeding tickets, and unlicensed vending at the festival, etc., Sheriff Hankins?" Preacher Mann asked.

"Since the County Beer Board gave a temporary permit for the Bluebird to sell beer at the fairgrounds on Friday and Saturday, we may have to deal with a few public drunks, too," Sheriff Hankins replied.

"Your lease says you can only sell beer on Friday and Saturday nights at the café, Cecil," Preacher Mann explained.

"I . . . er . . . uh . . . we amended the lease to include special events like the Mountain Music and Art Festival, the County Fair, and our Fourth of July celebration," George Hickman stammered.

"What was the Ferguson Merchants Association's position with the beer board?" the preacher asked the group.

"I took a letter to the beer board supporting the changes. It was signed by every businessperson in town and supported by Sheriff Hankins, too," Miss Rosie reported.

"I'm not happy about this. I think selling alcoholic beverages for Ferguson's special events is a mistake. I'm disappointed," Preacher Mann said.

"That's why we did it without your knowledge," the county nurse said.

"By saying we, do mean you were a part of this sordid conspiracy, Nellie Elizabeth Bilbrey-Mann?" the preacher asked with a slightly raised voice.

"Actually, I wrote a separate letter in support of the application and the position of the Ferguson Merchants Association," Nurse Mann responded in a quiet dignified tone.

"The beer is only about 4-5% alcohol," Dr. Whitman said, as he neared the large round dining table.

"Well, rat poison is 98% cornmeal and two-percent poison, but that two-percent gets the rat every time," Preacher Mann suggested with a snarl.

"Preacher, what's the difference in selling a little beer on Friday and Saturday nights and selling a little beer on a few special celebration days?" Cecil Smith asked.

"Kids! The difference is kids. When you turn the Bluebird Café into a nighttime honkytonk, there are no kids there to watch the drinking and resulting behavior. Now you've turned fun family events into drinking parties that expose children of all ages to adult behavior," Preacher Mann suggested.

"Now, Tom, let's be reasonable . . .," Nurse Mann began before being abruptly interrupted by the preacher.

"Reasonable! Reasonable! It seems the collective intelligence of the Ferguson business community plummets when they get fixated on chasing that next dollar!" the preacher exclaimed before he left the meeting.

"He's upset," Miss Rosie remarked.

"This is way beyond upset," Nurse Mann opined.

"He raises a good point," Dr. Marcus Whitman said.

Before anyone could respond, Preacher Mann returned to the large dining table and seated himself. His demeanor was much calmer, which was a relief to everyone present.

"Look, I've got a few suggestions. First, there will be no open beer cans or bottles outside the Bluebird Café, or outside the food tent at the County Fairgrounds. That's for the Music and Art Festival

and the County Fair. We can debate the issue further
after the festival," Preacher Mann remarked.

"What are your other suggestions, Brother Mann?"
Miss Ruby asked.

"Second, Ferguson is not a theocracy. I'm not the
appointed piety police officer. If it is the consensus of
the town's leadership that changes are needed, it is
not my duty to stand in the way. However, I suggest
you at least permit me to give counsel when serious
changes are contemplated," the preacher suggested.

"A wise man listens to counsel," Jack Wright
remarked.

"I like that. Who said that?" George Hickman
asked.

"The preacher, in a sermon a few months ago," the
merchant replied.

"Solomon in Proverbs 12:15," the preacher replied.

"I think we should follow all of Preacher Mann's
recommendations on this matter," Miss Rosie said.

"I second that," Miss Ruby responded.

"All in favor, raise their right hand," Louis Barrett
said.

"Looks like it is unanimous, preacher," Sheriff
Hankins reported.

"Well, I still don't like it, but I'll live with it," the
preacher retorted.

"What about the city judge's job?" Nurse Mann
asked.

"What's the pay?" the preacher asked.

"You want pay? You've got a job," the county nurse insisted.

"Well, it's $10 a day for two days, to be paid by the Ferguson Merchants Association to the Tennessee Christian Academy. That's about one-dollar a day for each merchant for each day," Preacher Mann proposed.

"Done deal," Louis Barrett said.

"This is a temporary appointment. You need to get one of the Cookeville lawyers to be the once-a-month and special- events city judge.

"Will do," Louis Barrett promised.

"So where does the city judge preside? At the meetinghouse?" the preacher asked.

"No, the Community Church property is being used on Friday and Saturday," Nurse Mann replied.

"Used for what?" the preacher asked with a slight degree of concern.

"A first aid station and a water ministry," the nurse said.

"What kind of ministry is a water ministry? Who approved the church as a first aid station?" Preacher Mann asked in rapid succession.

"Community Church's Minister of Education, Josh Sullivan. The first aid station is being staffed by Nurse Abby and Nurse Mann. The water ministry is being done by Brother Josh," the county nurse explained.

"Once again, what is a water ministry?" Preacher Mann insisted.

"A few weeks ago, you preached a sermon that said Jesus promised, 'For whosoever shall give you a cup of cold water to drink in my name . . . shall not lose his reward.' Looks like Josh took the message to heart and he's giving out cups of the 55-degree church well-water and brochures about Tennessee Christian Academy," Jack Wright explained.

"He will need hundreds of cups and brochures. Where does he plan on getting the money?" Preacher Mann inquired.

"He had me call Henry Wooden and he agreed to furnish ten cartons of 100 large cups each and a special donation of $20 to the academy. A portion of that money will pay for the paper and ink for the brochures," Jack Wright reported.

"I can't believe he worked a deal with Henry Wooden behind my back," the preacher said.

"He learned from the best," George Hickman remarked.

"You can set up in one of the tents at the fairgrounds. I doubt you'll have anything to do. You can judge the clogging, gospel music, and mountain art competitions. I don't think you'll be doing much as temporary city judge," Sheriff Hankins said.

By the end of the week, Ferguson was bustling with excitement. Most vendors, exhibitors, and musicians arrived very early to be ready for the beginning of the festival at 1:00 pm.

Based upon the attendance of the previous two county fairs, Sheriff Hankins estimated the crowd should swell to almost 500 attendees or more per day. If the weather held up, the Mountain Music and Art Festival would be another exciting and profitable endeavor for Ferguson.

About 12:30 pm, preacher man was seated beneath the contest judges' tent waiting for the contestants to arrive and the clogging event to begin. He heard a familiar voice call his name.

"Preacher, Preacher, I need to ask you a question," the voice said.

"What can I help you with SheMammy?" the preacher inquired.

"I'm the only person registered for the clogging contest. Can I clog while Doris Smith sings a gospel song?" SheMammy asked.

"What's the song?" the preacher queried.

"It's called 'Traveling the Highway Home' or 'Highway Home' I think. It's a good clogging tune," SheMammy explained.

"I'd say if it's spirit-filled, if it constitutes good clogging, and if lightning doesn't strike you, the Lord approves it," Preacher Mann replied.

"That's quite reassuring. Yes, that's very reassuring," Clayton Martin replied with slight sarcasm in his voice.

"SheMammy, we're told when the Ark of the Covenant returned to Jerusalem, David danced before the Lord with all his might. It probably was a gospel tune," the preacher said.

"I like that answer better. Now *that* is reassuring," SheMammy remarked.

As the preacher watched, SheMammy Martin, clad in a red and black, long sleeve, cotton work shirt and a pair of overalls, met Doris Smith and the Smith Brothers on the makeshift stage.

The gospel singing competition centered on Doris' performance, as the Smith Brothers Band was the accompaniment for all gospel singing competitors. SheMammy must clog, or flat foot dance, in rhythm to the instrumental accompaniment.

The Smith Brothers began the song, "Highway Home," with a short musical introduction. At the appropriate time Doris Smith sang:

> **"Traveling the highway home**
> **I'm traveling the highway home**
> **Oh narrow's the way, thank God I can say**
> **I'm traveling the highway home."**

The preacher noted Doris' pitch and timing were perfect. It was obvious she'd sung quite a few gospel songs with the Smith Brothers in their travels.

By the second stanza, the preacher focused intently on the click made by the heel and toe taps on SheMammy's work shoes. He was keeping perfect rhythm.

The preacher thought to himself he was probably giving King David a run for his money, clogging to that gospel tune.

SheMammy danced enthusiastically and Doris sang emphatically:

> **"Well ol' Satan said that I'd never be**
> **Traveling the highway home**
> **When I resisted, he had to flee**
> **I'm traveling the highway home."**

Although the winners wouldn't be announced until later that day, SheMammy had clinched the Clogging Championship at Ferguson's First Annual Mountain Music and Art Festival. Doris barely won the Gospel Singing Championship as Marilyn Mitchell and the Little Mitchell girls gave a near-perfect performance of the Carter Family tune, "On the Sea Of Galilee." The Mitchells finished a very close second.

\*     \*     \*

There was no criminal conduct or cases for the newly appointed municipal judge to decide on the first day of the festival. In fact, neither Sheriff Hankins nor any of his deputies felt it necessary to even give a warning to any of the patrons.

Nurse Abby and Nurse Mann had an eventful day at the first aid station positioned at Community Church. They treated one skinned knee, one bee sting, and a blister on the finger of an upright bass player in one of the bands.

Before the preacher could begin his Saturday afternoon rounds to consider the various entries in the mountain art/painting category, Sheriff Hankins appeared at the tent and motioned for the preacher to come with him.

"What's the problem?" Preacher Mann asked.

"You'll find out," Sheriff Hankins said gruffly.

"Are you the city judge?" a young vendor queried.

"Yes," the preacher replied.

"Are you a preacher, too?" the young man asked.

"Yes," the preacher answered.

"I'm headed for the gallows," the young man lamented.

"What's the problem, sheriff?" Preacher Mann queried.

"He's displaying and selling postcards and paintings of indecently exposed women, in violation of Tennessee's obscenity laws," Sheriff Hankins said.

"What specific conduct are you alleging that constitutes a violation?" the new city judge asked.

"He's exhibiting, possessing, and offering for sale obscene materials," the sheriff replied.

"All I sell is art. It is not obscenity," the young man objected.

"Close the doorway of your tent and show me what you're selling or trying to sell," the preacher said.

"Why?" the vendor asked.

"If you happen to be guilty, I don't want the sheriff to add a charge of displaying the obscene materials to minors," Preacher Mann explained.

The young man handed four boxes of pencil-drawn, printed postcards to the preacher. The first two boxes contained two different drawings of young women sitting on a bed and facing away from the artist. She was obviously topless, combing her hair, and had a partially bare bottom slightly covered by a bedsheet.

"These drawings do not meet the definition of obscenity under Tennessee law. Sheriff Hankins could, under your vendor agreement with the Ferguson Merchants Association, terminate your participation and require you to leave the festival. I recommend against that, but that's his call.

"Here are the other cards," the vendor said as he handed the boxes to the preacher.

The final two boxes contained pencil drawings of a young naked woman facing the artist. She was sitting crossed-legged in one drawing, with hands on her knees. She was displaying her bare breasts, but her genitals were not visible.

In the second drawing, the woman was lounging naked on a bed propping herself up on one arm. Her breasts and naked body were fully displayed but she was turned in such a way her top leg slighted covered her pubic area.

"Let me ask you a few questions which may or may not be relevant to my decision," the preacher said.

"I'll answer everything truthfully," the vendor said.

"How much are these cards?" the preacher inquired.

"They are 25 cents each or three for a dollar," the vendor said.

"Are you related to Ches McCartney?" the preacher asked, as he and Sheriff Hankins started to laugh.

"Not that I know. My name is Charlie Cole, Jr. I'm originally from Alabama but I'm going to school at the University of Tennessee. I'm off for the summer," young Cole responded.

"Are you the artist on these pencil drawings?" Sheriff Hankins queried.

"No, sir. The original drawings were canvas pencil drawings done by my father. I had a printer reduce them to postcard size to sell to help me with school expenses," Charlie Cole asked.

"Who was the printer?" Sheriff Hankins asked.

"It was one of my classmates. His name is Lynn Malone, but I don't want to get him in trouble. We printed them at the school print lab," the young man answered.

"What is your cost for printing these two boxes of cards?" the preacher asked.

"It's about three cents a card or less for the 200 cards. That's about six dollars, but it's probably closer to five dollars," Charlie Cole replied.

"Have you actually sold any of these two types of cards?" the preacher asked.

"I sold about fifty from the first two boxes but not any from these two. I've made about $20 for the two days," young Cole announced with a smile.

"These cards are close to being obscene in that they tend to show a portion of the pubic area and are dangerously close to showing a portion of the female genitalia. But after a careful look, they are not obscene," the preacher stated.

"Whew! That's great," Charlie Cole said.

"There is one problem with these cards," Preacher Mann said.

"Tell me. I want to know. I won't sell them," young Cole pleaded.

"You are using the naked image of a woman that shows her face. That's called invasion of privacy since she's not a public figure. It's a civil matter but not a criminal issue," Preacher Mann explained.

"Who's the woman? How do we deal with that?' Sheriff Hankins inquired.

"Take a closer look. You know the woman. Go round her up for us," Preacher Mann instructed.

"We're going to permit you to make one last sale before you agree to never print or distribute these two drawings again," the preacher explained.

Just as he finished his instructions, Sheriff Hankins arrived with Nurse Beth Bilbrey-Mann. She had a strange look on her face.

"It's her. It's the woman," Charlie Cole announced excitedly.

"This is Charlie Cole, Jr. He's from Birmingham. He's a student at UT. His father is an artist. He's selling pencil drawing cards to help make his way through school," Preacher Mann announced.

"How does that affect me?" the county nurse inquired.

Preacher Mann handed the two boxes of cards to her, and she turned white. She looked at Preacher Mann and then at Charlie Cole.

"Is your father Charles Dubois "Bo" Cole?" the nurse asked.

"Tom . . . I . . . uh . . . I mean," Nurse Mann explained.

"Beth, Charlie has agreed to no longer invade your privacy by printing, distributing, or selling these particular cards. But he has incurred six dollars in expenses in producing these cards," the preacher explained.

"I'm not giving him six dollars for illegally selling nude drawings of me!" Nurse Mann exclaimed.

"The six dollars is for him. But it's a bribe to keep the municipal judge and the county sheriff from ever telling anyone about this, or asking them if they've heard about it," Preacher Mann explained.

Nurse Mann reached into her purse and handed six crisp one-dollar bills to Charlie Cole. She took the two boxes of improper cards and shoved them into her purse.

"This is because of that beer board letter," she said with indignation.

"Consider it as beer money," Preacher Mann said as he and Sheriff Hankins began to belly laugh.

When he regained his composure, the preacher said, "Son, I would pack up and head back to Knoxville before you run into her. You might warn your Dad you almost got scorched by one of his old flames."

Charlie Cole nodded and started packing up his vendor tent. He wasted no time heading for Knoxville.

"You'll catch a trainload of grief over this, preacher," Sheriff Hankins said.

"She'll be quite gentle with me until she finds out whether or not I've got a set of those four postcards," Preacher Mann said.

"You didn't get a set," the sheriff remarked.

"Charlie nodded that I could have one each, from the first two boxes. When I nodded toward the last two boxes, he slipped out one each and discreetly handed them me before he gave her the boxes," Preacher Mann said.

"He sounds like a business major," Sheriff Hankins said with a loud laugh.

"Probably sales and marketing," Preacher Mann said with his own loud laugh.

# 4. Balm of Gilead

Jack Wright was helping sack a customer's groceries early on Saturday morning as the preacher and the county nurse arrived. Nurse Mann was wearing a pair of shorts with a blouse tied slightly above her waist.

Preacher Mann was wearing a pair of khaki work pants, a short sleeve light blue shirt, and a fishing vest. He looked more like a department store mannequin than a country fisherman.

"I'll be right with you," Jack Wright announced as he carried two bags of groceries to a lady's vehicle outside the store.

"He's busy," Nurse Mann said.

"It's his longest, busiest day of the week. I try to stay away from here most Saturdays," Preacher Mann explained.

"I thought it was because you wanted to spend some quiet time with me," the nurse suggested.

"Quiet would be my idea of how to spend the time," the preacher replied.

"I was speaking euphemistically," Nurse Mann explained.

"We need to work on our communication," Preacher Mann suggested.

"Indeed," the nurse responded.

Upon reentering the store, Jack Wright remarked, "I thought Monday was your day off, preacher."

"I swapped days with Brother Josh. My new off day is now Saturday," the preacher replied.

"What's the deal?" the merchant inquired.

"He's working with Louis and Patricia Barrett on Mondays, getting lesson booklets printed at the Mountain Gazette in the mornings, and grading completed lessons in the evenings," Preacher Mann said with a chuckle.

"How's the education ministry going for him?" Jack Wright asked.

"He's got over 100 students in over a dozen different classes at the academy. He spends two nights a week at the Barrett's doing the remainder of his education courses for Middle Tennessee State Teachers College," Preacher Mann said.

"I'm sorry I ignored you, Miss Beth. I get a lot of my news from the preacher," the storekeeper said apologetically.

"That's not a problem. He's the source of all my news, too," Nurse Mann said.

"But I never report any news involving the two of you," the preacher said with a chuckle.

"Yeah, it costs me lunch at least one day a week," Jack Wright remarked.

"Lunch? He made me pay six dollars to shut him up last week about the festival," the county nurse remarked.

"If it was that good, I can take up a collection and get your money back today," Jack Wright offered.

"I don't have a dog in this fight," Preacher Mann said with a huge smile.

"Be careful of the fight in the dog," the county nurse remarked.

Quickly changing the subject, Jack Wright asked, "Is there something you need for your outing today?"

"He needs a spool of nylon fishing line. He's taking his wife to the Crawdad Hole for fishing and picnicking," the nurse explained.

"I was hoping for cavorting, too," Preacher Mann remarked.

"That's not out of the question," the county nurse replied.

"Your secret's safe with me. I've sworn off gossip altogether," Jack Wright exclaimed.

"What's the secret?" Louis Barrett said as he walked to the back of Discount Grocery.

"We're going to the Crawdad Hole to engage in some cavorting," Nurse Mann reported.

"That's not gossip. You're married to each other," the newspaper editor opined.

"Once your romance buds, it flowers, and eventually hits full bloom, you immediately become old news," Preacher Mann replied.

"I hope so," Nurse Mann said with a chuckle.

"I'll pay for the fishing line, Brother Jack. It's getting toward cavorting time," the preacher instructed.

Feeling inspired Jack Wright begins crooning a line from the "Crawdad Song:"

> **"You get a line. I'll get a pole, honey**
> **You get a line. I'll get a pole, babe.**
> **You get a line. I'll get a pole**
> **We'll go down to the crawdad hole**
> **Honey, babe of mine."**

"He'll never make the Smith Brothers Band," Louis Barrett said, looking toward the preacher.

"We're leaving before the Sheriff shows up thinking a coyote is loose in town," the preacher replied as he and his wife walked toward with store.

"Everyone's a music critic," Jack Wright exclaimed.

\*      \*      \*

Just as the preacher and the county nurse started to get into the preacher's old, black Ford truck, Brother Josh appeared in a rather excited state. The pair knew something was amiss.

"Preacher, you've got to go to Buck Mountain to see Ridley Fleming. It's important," Josh Sullivan implored.

"What's the problem?" Preacher Mann asked.

"He hasn't eaten anything in days. He won't talk to his wife. He just sits and holds his old bluetick hound that's dead," Josh explained.

"Really Josh? You can't deal with a depressed man who's lost a family pet?" Nurse Mann chided.

"Barbara Fleming sent word down from Buck Mountain by one of the miners. She asked specifically for Preacher Mann. I'll go, too," the young minister said.

"Hop in the back of the truck. We are going to Buck Mountain," Preacher Mann announced.

On the way up the mountain, Nurse Mann inquired, "Do you really think it's this serious?"

"A dog is the only thing in life that loves a man more than the man loves himself. Losing Ol' Blue is tantamount to losing the best friend Ridley Fleming ever had," Preacher Mann responded.

When they arrived at the Fleming cabin atop Buck Mountain, Barbara Fleming gave the preacher a teary-eyed hug. In a broken voice, she thanked him for coming.

"What's the situation?" the preacher inquired.

"Three days ago, our two-year-old, Rudy, wandered away from the cabin. We searched and

51

searched but couldn't find him. Ol' Blue went missing, too. The toddler and the dog got along, but they mostly stayed clear of each other after Rudy pulled his ears and the dog growled and snapped at him a few months ago.

In a few hours, the dog came back to the yard. He had blood all over him. Ridley just knew the dog had chewed up the kid, so he grabbed his rifle. He shot and killed the dog.

I followed the blood tracks to about 75 feet west of here. Rudy was sitting near a large, grey wolf. It had obviously been killed by Ol' Blue to protect the baby.

Ridley went back to the cabin, picked up Ol' Blue, and took him to the back porch. He's been there ever since. He has drunk a little water, but he won't eat. He just sits there petting that old hound's body."

"He's suffering from severe clinical depression. He needs medical help," the county nurse opined.

"I'll talk to him. You two can join me, but let me do the talking," the preacher instructed.

"You think you can do any good?" Brother Josh asked.

Quoting from an old hymn entitled: "There Is A Balm in Gilead", Preacher Mann said:

**"There is a balm in Gilead**
**To make the wounded whole**
**There is a balm in Gilead**
**To heal the sin-sick soul."**

Barbara Fleming led the two preachers and the county nurse around the end of the cabin and to the back porch. Ridley had positioned himself against the back wall and held Ol' Blue's bloody head in his lap.

Ridley Fleming looked at Preacher Mann and asked pointedly, "Do dogs go to heaven?"

"Will Rogers once said, 'If there are no dogs in heaven, then when I die, I want to go where they're at,'" the preacher answered.

"I guess the wife told you what happened," Ridley Fleming said.

"She said you mistakenly shot Ol' Blue out of anguish that he attacked Rudy," the preacher replied.

"It was anger. It was pure anger. That old dog saved my boy. I thought he killed that child. Ol' Blue looked at me and I shot him dead," Ridley Fleming said between sobs.

"I brought Brother Josh. He'll see Ol' Blue gets a proper burial. He'll say a few words for him, too," Preacher Mann explained.

Ridley looked at Brother Josh, gave a momentary smile, and said, "Much obliged."

Josh Sullivan gave an affirmative nod. Years later he wrote in his journal that he didn't say anything to Ridley Fleming because his voice had left him.

"Preacher, I'll never be able to forgive myself for what I've done," Mr. Fleming lamented.

"I knew a man who made a mistake that was so bad he couldn't forgive himself and he didn't believe even God would forgive him," Preacher Mann remarked.

"Say on," Ridley encouraged.

"The man worked in the Mobile shipyards. He built and repaired ships of all kinds. He was a master shipbuilder.

His hobby was catching rattlesnakes. He would hunt, kill, skin, and tan the hides of eastern diamondback rattlers. He sold them to a company that used the hides for belts, boots, wallets, purses, dress shoes, and other kinds of things.

One weekend he caught the largest rattlesnake he had ever seen. It was almost eight feet long and weighed 35 pounds," the preacher said.

"Damn! That's one big snake. Did he kill it and sell its hide?" Ridley inquired.

"Actually, he took it home and put it in a small wire and plywood, double rabbit cage. He intended to show it off. But after dark, his five-year-old son went to the cage to try to get the snake to shake its rattle.

The snake got very upset, struck at the child through the cage door, broke through the plywood, and sunk its teeth into the little boy," the preacher explained.

"Oh no," Nurse Mann gasped.

"Did he get him to the doctor? Were they able to save him?" Ridley Fleming asked.

"The father rushed from the house to the cage. He took an ax and killed the large snake, cutting it into several pieces. Unfortunately, the rattler had pumped his deadly venom into the child's abdomen. Little Danny died in his father's arms," Preacher Mann said in a faltering voice.

"What happened to the boy's dad?" Ridley Fleming intently inquired.

"It was days before the Dad would eat anything and weeks before he returned to work. He couldn't forgive himself and he believed God would never forgive him either. But, one day he changed his mind," the preacher replied.

"What changed his mind?" Ridley Fleming begged.

"His older son explained there was nothing too bad to cause God not to forgive us. He quoted him a Bible verse: I John 1:7," the preacher said.

Brother Josh began quoting, "But if we walk in the light, as he is in the light, we have fellowship one with another, and the blood of Jesus Christ his Son cleanseth us from *all* sin."

Ridley Fleming gently laid Ol' Blue's head onto the floor of the porch. He stood, dusted himself off, stepped toward Preacher Mann, and embraced him.

With tears in his eyes and still holding the preacher tightly, he said, "Preacher, you'll never know this side of heaven, what you've done for me."

Preacher Mann said softly, "The Lord did it. I just happened to be here."

"Brother Josh, will you take Ol' Blue to the front. Barbara can show you where the grave needs to be dug. I'll take care of that. I'd be obliged if you come by after services tomorrow and say some nice things about that old bluetick hound," Ridley Fleming requested.

"I'll be here at about 11:30 am," Brother Josh replied.

"Preacher, we're sorry to interrupt your fishing trip," Barbara Fleming lamented.

"I'm glad you did," Preacher Mann said.

"I am glad, too," Nurse Mann remarked.

"Mr. Fleming, let me dig Old Blue's grave. You need to clean up and take some food," Brother Josh suggested.

"Don't argue with him, Ridley. Young preachers are more hard-headed than old preachers," Preacher Mann said with a smile.

"Well, it's two against one. Once you get around front, I'll fill the washtub and do the needful," Ridley Fleming promised.

*      *      *

Once Brother Josh dug Ol' Blues grave, he and Barbara wrapped the old hound in a worn quilt and tied it with sisal twine. They paused for a moment before proceeding further.

They gently and reverently lowered him into the three-foot-deep grave. Josh carefully covered the grave and then packed the soil firmly.

On the way down the mountain, Brother Josh asked, "Preacher Mann, did you know that snake hunter and his family?"

"Indeed," the preacher replied.

"Were they neighbors? Were they family friends? Were they church members?" Nurse Mann asked in rapid succession.

"The snake hunter was my father. Little Danny was my five-year-old brother. I was twelve years old when I quoted my father the Bible verse. I guess that's one reason why my father always wanted me to be a preacher," Preacher Mann said.

Brother Josh Sullivan said, among other things, 'The Lord hath anointed you to . . . bind up the brokenhearted.'"

Nurse Mann said, "Amen."

## 5. Love Child

Nurse Mann woke up the preacher around midnight after hearing what seemed to be an angry quarrel in the hallway outside their room. She heard the exchange but couldn't discern the nature of the argument.

It ended with Miss Rosie screaming, "If you don't get the hell out of here, I'll have Sheriff Hankins put you under the damn jail."

By the time Nurse Mann got the preacher awake, had him don his pants, and sent him into the hallway to check on the verbal altercation, it had already concluded.

"What did you see?" the county nurse asked as the preacher returned to their room.

"Not much," Preacher Mann replied.

"Well, who was there?" she inquired with a slight degree of irritation.

"I saw Miss Rosie headed down the stairs. She was alone," the preacher responded.

"What do you intend to do?" Nurse Mann asked.

"Make passionate love to you," the preacher said flatly.

"Really?" the county nurse remarked.

"No, I'm going to bed and going back to sleep," the preacher explained, as he headed toward the large iron bed.

"Why aren't you going to find out what's going on?" Nurse Mann inquired.

"But let none of you suffer . . . as a busybody in other men's matters," the preacher said quoting from I Peter 4:15.

"You think checking on someone in a shouting match is being a busybody?" the nurse asked indignantly.

Quoting from Proverbs 20:3 the preacher said, "It is an honor for a man to cease from strife: but every fool will be meddling."

Nurse Mann returned to the large iron bed, turned away from Preacher Mann, and pulled the covers over her without saying anything.

The preacher said nothing either. But it's a good thing the room was dark, and his wife couldn't see his ear-to-ear smile.

The next morning, the preacher and his wife decided to have a quick breakfast before they began their Monday routine. On that particular day, Nurse Mann was working at the western end of Putnam County making calls on patients in Cookeville, Baxter, and near the DeKalb County line. The preacher promised to help Brother Josh Sullivan grade Bible lessons from students enrolled in the academy.

The couple seated themselves at one of the white tablecloth-covered tables in the large dining room at Miss Rosie's. It wasn't long before she came to the table with her pencil and order pad.

"What can I get for you, Nurse Mann?" Miss Rosie asked with a smile.

"I'm in Cookeville and as far as the western part of the county today. I need to hurry. Just give me an order of toast and a small bowl of oatmeal," the county nurse replied.

"I know your order, preacher. It's two country ham biscuits and a Coca-Cola," Miss Rosie opined.

"That's exactly what I want. But I can't figure out how you knew that," Preacher Mann said with a puzzled look.

"On the days Nurse Mann works the west end of the county, you always have two country ham biscuits and a Coke," Miss Rosie replied.

"Tom, why do you do that?" Nurse Mann asked.

"I don't want to delay your drive to Cookeville. It's a good half-hour commute to your first visit," Preacher Mann responded.

"He's considerate. He cares about his wife. He's not like the jackass I had to put out of here last night," Miss Rosie said with a louder than normal voice.

"What happened? We heard the commotion and…," Nurse Mann said before being interrupted by the Preacher's coughing spell.

"I'll get him some water. We can talk about it tonight," Miss Rosie said as she headed toward the kitchen.

"That was quite a strategic coughing spell," Nurse Mann remarked.

"Indeed," Preacher Mann said.

"If there's a problem, you need to tell me plainly," Nurse Mann said.

"I told you last night," the preacher retorted.

Miss Rosie returned to the table, followed by Anna Mae Crowder Whitman. The two women were carrying the orders and the drinks.

Seeking to avoid any further discussion, the preacher carefully wrapped up his two country ham biscuits in a cloth napkin. He picked up the bottle of Coca-Cola in the other hand.

"I'll see you tonight. Have a pleasant day, Elizabeth," the preacher said as he made his way through the large dining room and out the front door.

Anna Mae's presence warranted further inquiry but after Preacher Mann's commentary about meddling and busybodies, the county nurse decided to avoid the issue entirely.

The preacher made his way down the street to eat his breakfast at Discount Grocery. He had his wrapped country ham biscuits in one hand and his soft drink in the other.

Seeing Preacher Mann enter the store, Jack Wright remarked, "Preacher, that's so thoughtful of you but I've already had a huge breakfast today."

"Good," the preacher grunted.

"You're out really early. What's going on?" the merchant inquired.

"Breakfast," the preacher said after taking his first bite.

"You're Grumpy," Jack Wright said referencing the recently released RKO Pictures movie, Snow White and the Seven Dwarfs.

"You've spent too much time at the magic mirror," Preacher Mann retorted sharply.

"That was harsh," Louis Barrett said as he walked toward the back of the store.

"He's like a starving dog going after those country ham biscuits. He'll growl at you until he's filled his belly," Jack Wright remarked.

Deciding to change the subject, Louis Barrett said, "I heard our beloved Dr. Marcus Whitman and his wife had the argument of the century at midnight at Miss Rosie's until she threatened to call the law on him."

"What were they doing fighting at Miss Rosie's at midnight?" Jack Wright asked.

"Apparently, she decided to pack a bag and relocate temporarily to the bed and breakfast. He followed her over and the confrontation occurred," Louis Barrett reported.

"I wonder what caused the blow-up?" Jack Wright mused.

"Just call Marcus on the phone and ask him. It'll cut out all this gossiping," Preacher Mann suggested.

Louis Barrett and Jack Wright hung their heads and looked toward the floor. Neither of them said a word in response to the preacher's slight chastisement.

After what seemed to be an eternity, the phone rang, and Jack Wright moved to answer it. He listened briefly before responding.

"He's here. I'll tell him right now," Jack Wright promised before hanging up the phone.

"Dr. Whitman said to tell you he needed to talk to you. He said it was important," Jack Wright reported.

The preacher nodded. When he finished his breakfast, he nodded, walked to the front of the store, and left.

"He hates gossip or people that meddle in other folks' business," Jack Wright said.

"He knows it doesn't take much to cause strife and unnecessary controversy," Louis Barrett said.

"That's why he's the preacher and we're not," the merchant said with a smile.

Preacher Mann walked through the front door of
Scott's Apothecary to the noise of a little bell that
jingles and announces a customer's arrival. Without
speaking, Joe Scott held up his right index finger
indicating for the preacher to give him one minute to
retrieve Dr. Whitman.

He returned with Dr. Marcus Whitman. They both
nodded toward the storage room. Preacher Mann
walked to the back of the drug store.

Once safely inside the storeroom, Dr. Whitman
closed the door. He had a very sad demeanor and had
difficulty discussing his situation with the preacher.

"I guess you know about the huge argument last
night at Miss Rosie's," Dr. Whitman remarked.

"I heard a muffled argument. I didn't know the
identity of the parties. I didn't inquire about it from
Miss Rosie," Preacher Mann replied.

"Well, she gave me the choice of leaving or going
to jail," the physician explained.

"What caused the argument?" Preacher Mann
queried.

"Two days ago an old girlfriend showed up at the
clinic and sought me out," Dr. Whitman said.

"Wives generally don't take kindly to visits from
old flames," the preacher opined.

65

"It gets worse. She had her three-year-old son with her, and she claimed he was our love child," the doctor added.

"Were you aware of the child's existence?" the preacher queried.

"I had a serious romantic relationship with her, but it ended about a year before you and I met. I was unaware of the pregnancy," Dr. Whitman explained.

"Why do you think she showed up this much later?" Preacher Mann queried.

"She said she came to realize Jason needed both a dad and a mom and she'd been wrong to exclude me," the doctor replied.

"Is that when Anna Mae became upset?" the preacher inquired.

"Actually, she took the news pretty well. Since she's less than two months from delivering our child, she was somewhat sympathetic to Janice's plight and Jason's situation," Dr. Whitman reported.

"What do you think caused the change of heart?" the preacher queried.

"She was in good spirits most of Saturday. By Sunday afternoon, she was verbally abusive about whether I was still in love with Janice and whether I married her because Janice wouldn't have me. Eventually, she packed a bag on Sunday night and headed to Miss Rosie's," the physician explained.

"How are you handling this situation?" the preacher queried.

"I'm like that man in the song "I Can't Even Walk" that Marilyn Mitchell sings:

**"I thought I could do a lot on my own
I thought I could make it all day long
I thought of myself as a mighty big man
But I can't even walk without you holding my
hand."**

"What do you need me to do?" Preacher Mann asked.

"We're at an impasse. She's headed to a lawyer in Cookeville and said she's filing for divorce. I need you to reason with her. She'll listen to you," Dr. Whitman explained.

"I'll let her calm down today and talk to her tomorrow. I need to find out what provoked her after her initial support for the mother and child," the preacher replied.

"Do you have any advice for me?" the doctor asked.

"Keep doing your job. Pray. Keep your mouth shut. We don't need any tongues wagging to upset her further," Preacher Mann instructed.

"I'll do just that," Dr. Whitman promised.

Preacher Mann nodded and opened the storeroom door. He made his way through the apothecary lobby, past the lunch counter, and walked through the front door without saying a word.

*       *       *

The preacher made his way to the Mountain Gazette office and began grading correspondence lessons while Brother Josh Sullivan and Louis Barrett printed lesson booklets for students of Tennessee Christian Academy.

"Josh, I have an issue to discuss with you," Preacher Mann said

"Say on," Josh replied.

"Wait a minute. I've got a question before you two get started. Why do both of you often reply, 'Say on' in a conversation?" the newspaper editor asked.

"When Jesus was eating a meal at the house of Simon, the Pharisee, a sinful woman bathed his feet with her tears and anointed him with a box of expensive ointment. Simon thought Jesus shouldn't even be letting the woman touch him.

Knowing his thoughts, Jesus said, 'Simon, I have somewhat to say unto thee.' And Simon said, 'Master, say on,'" Brother Josh explained.

"So, when it's a serious question being asked or a point being made, Preacher Mann says, 'Say on,'" Louis Barrett mused.

"Now that *that's* resolved, say on, Preacher Mann," Brother Josh instructed.

"Why is it that the preacher is working for the assistant preacher?" Preacher Mann asked.

"It's because I'm only the assistant. You're reviewing our Bible coursework and grading the student's response to ensure we're doing things right," Brother Josh explained.

"Are you sure you weren't taking a few classes at Vanderbilt Law School, too?" Louis Barrett asked with a chuckle.

"After a few more days, when you two have caught up on printing, you'll get your final approval from me," Preacher Mann promised.

"Sounds like he's ours for the rest of this week," Louis Barrett opined.

"Say on!" Brother Josh exclaimed.

\*     \*     \*

When Preacher Mann returned to Miss Rosie's Bed & Breakfast, he made arrangements for Wednesday morning to talk with Anna Mae Whitman. She was willing to speak with Preacher Mann, but she made her intentions clear regarding the divorce.

When Nurse Mann returned from her day's rural health care visits, Miss Rosie appeared with Anna Mae Whitman in tow. Before any of the women could speak, Preacher Mann surprised them with an announcement.

"Brother Josh and Louis Barrett are sorting and assembling lessons for the correspondence high school in the meetinghouse auditorium for the next few days. Miss Rosie, I need to hold the regular Wednesday evening prayer meeting here this week," Preacher Mann announced.

"We're always available for the Lord's work," Miss Rosie replied.

"I forgot to mention Marilyn Mitchell will be doing a song or two with the Smith Brothers Band at the end," he further explained.

"I'll have the cook whip up some extra dinner specials for the crowd," Miss Rosie promised.

"Is there something you two needed?" the preacher inquired.

"Now preacher, Anna Mae is shy. She knows you're going to try to talk her into going back with that womanizing husband of hers. That's not a problem because that's your job. But you're wasting your time trying to help that fornicator. It won't work," Miss Rosie said.

"I found a stack of her old love letters that he had saved. He'd hid them in a trunk in the attic," Anna Mae added.

"That's just terrible," Nurse Mann remarked as the two other women nodded affirmatively.

"I think that's a very harsh position you three are taking," Preacher Mann said.

"Harsh in what way? Explain yourself." Miss Rosie insisted indignantly.

"It's fairly self-righteous coming from a woman that used to run a whorehouse, and a whore who worked for her," Preacher Mann said bluntly.

"I can't believe you'd say that to us. That's outrageous!" Miss Rosie exclaimed.

"Jesus warned, 'For with what judgment ye judge, ye shall be judged.' If you want to look at the old indiscretions of Dr. Marcus Whitman, I think there's a warning that the same standard would be appropriate for the two of you," Preacher Mann said flatly.

Miss Rosie and Anna Mae spun on their heels and made a beeline out of the parlor toward the kitchen. The preacher would later write in his journal that they took off like two old cats whose tails had been caught in the rockers of a rocking chair.

"You offended them," Nurse Mann exclaimed.

"Jesus offended them. They can take it up with Him. I'm just the messenger," Preacher Mann exclaimed.

"Well, I happen to think they are right," Nurse Mann said smugly.

"I'd be careful about making judgments about Dr. Whitman's past indiscretions, too," the preacher replied.

"Say on," the county nurse suggested.

"About two weeks ago, the son of one of your old flames showed up with prints of naked drawings you posed for. You and I both know it took a while for him to do those drawings.

You were nude, sitting on a bed, and only partially wrapped in a bedsheet. I didn't engage in speculation, leave our marriage bed, start a public verbal altercation, or threaten a divorce.

If you want to judge Dr. Whitman harshly, it's fair for others to apply the same standard – even me," Preacher Mann opined.

There was a long pause before either of them spoke. The county nurse looked tearfully at the preacher when she opted to speak.

"I made a mistake back then and I made a mistake today. I will not make those mistakes again," Nurse Mann said.

"It's hard to be a good preacher, a good husband, and a good friend to a congregation and a wife. But that's the duties I have chosen in life. I don't regret any of them," Preacher Mann replied.

*     *     *

The following evening a larger than usual crowd appeared for dinner at Miss Rosie's, listened a few minutes of the preacher's devotion, and experienced a short gospel music show by the Smith Brothers Band.

Preacher Mann stepped to the lectern and said, "Tonight's devotional message is being delivered by Miss Marilyn Mitchell in a song called, 'You Don't Love God If You Don't Love Your Neighbor.'"

Miss Rosie and Anna Mae always said Preacher Mann's rebuke, coupled with the second verse of that song, convicted them and caused them to change their attitude toward Dr. Marcus Whitman and others they would encounter in life,

It said in pertinent part:

**"In the Holy Bible, in the book of Matthew**
**Read the 18th Chapter and the 21st verse**
**Jesus plainly tells us that we must have mercy**
**There's a special warning in the 35th verse.**
**Oh you don't love God**
**If you don't love your neighbor**
**If you gossip about him, if you never have mercy**
**If he gets into trouble, and you don't try to help him**
**Then you don't love your neighbor**
**And you don't love God."**

After the service, Anna Mae packed her bag and went home with Dr. Marcus Whitman. When Jason came for a visit, she acted more like a mother than a stepmother. Jason eventually became a big brother to the children of Anna Mae and Dr. Whitman.

A teary-eyed Miss Rosie hugged the preacher firmly and whispered in his ear, "I love you, preacher. You're the real deal."

Neither Preacher Mann nor Nurse Mann ever spoke again of the erotic artwork. In fact, the county nurse became an enemy of gossip and an advocate for the miracle of forgiveness.

Louis Barrett never again printed a gossip column in The Mountain Gazette.

Jack Wright said if gossip ever started in his presence, he was going to cover his ears and refuse to listen just like SheMammy.

Preacher Mann would write in his journal that it was the only sermon that he got credit for preaching, but he had preached vicariously.

# 6. Thanksgiving

Nurse Mann looked at her wristwatch and asked, "Tom, what time did George Hickman and Finis Martin say they'd be here?"

"George left a message with Miss Rosie for us to meet them at Simpson Meadows promptly at 8:30 am," Preacher Mann replied.

"Well, it's after 9:00 am and nobody's here. How long do you intend to wait on them?" the county nurse inquired.

"I figure they'll be here by 9:30 am. If not, we'll jump in the truck and head over to Hickman Bank," Preacher Mann promised.

Before Nurse Mann could reply, George Hickman pulled his old 1929 Ford pickup truck into the cul-de-sac at Simpson Meadows. Finis Lawrence was sitting in the passenger seat.

As they exited the truck, George Hickman remarked, "I'm sorry we're a little late. I was getting a construction update from Finis."

"What's the verdict?" the preacher asked.

"It's good news. He plans on having all three of these houses completed before the year's end.

Weather permitting, he hopes to start on the next three homes shortly thereafter," George Hickman announced.

"Why did you need us this morning? We could have gotten your update by telephone," Nurse Mann suggested.

"I need you to pick out some colors, flooring, and window treatments for your new home," Finis Lawrence replied.

"Which home is ours?" the county nurse inquired.

"Any one you want. You get the pick of the litter," George Hickman announced.

"George, you just tripled this morning's work," Preacher Mann said.

"Why would you say that?" the banker queried.

"Because Tom knows I will need to tour all three houses before deciding," Nurse Mann said, as she walked with Finis Lawrence toward the center house.

"Aren't you taking the nickel tour, preacher?" Finish Lawrence asked.

"I need him for a few minutes. We've got some business to discuss," George Hickman said.

Once Nurse Mann and Finis Lawrence made their way into the first Simpson Meadows home, George Hickman said, "Preacher, I've got a deal for you. It'll help me, and it'll make you a hero with your wife."

"Say on," Preacher Mann replied.

"I need to delay your moving into one of these houses until about mid-February. I know it will be an inconvenience. I've worked out a deal with Finis Lawrence to provide the new furniture to fully furnish every room in the house to your wife's satisfaction.

I'll add the total to the lease-purchase price. If you move, the furniture stays with the house. If you eventually opt for purchase, it's yours," the banker explained.

"What if I move and want to take the furniture to a new city?" Preacher Mann inquired.

"I'll sell it to you at cost," George Hickman promised.

"Shake my hand and put it in the paperwork. But I only have one concern," the preacher replied.

"What's your concern?" the banker asked with a serious tone.

"I'm afraid I've broken your spirit. You are making deals with me that are so good I'm ashamed to try to negotiate with you," Preacher Mann said with a laugh.

"What's that verse about casting your bread on the water?" the banker asked.

"It's Ecclesiastes 11:1 and it says, 'Cast thy bread upon the waters: for after many days thou shalt find it,'" Preacher Mann responded.

"Preacher you said it means that if you do something kind for someone, without expecting a return, God will reward you," George Hickman responded.

"That's right. Blessings will be returned to those who are kind and generous," Preacher Mann opined.

"Let's not start saying George Hickman, the banker, is kind and generous. But I can see how having a fully-furnished model home for six weeks will help sell three more homes by the time Finis Lawrence gets them finished," George Hickman replied with a chuckle.

"I won't tell it, but I may ask a few folks if they know about it," Preacher Mann said with a smile.

"I've looked at all three houses and picked the one I like," Nurse Mann reported.

"Which one did you choose?" the preacher queried.

"I picked the one in the center," she announced.

"That's the largest one," the banker remarked.

"Better get a few more loaves of bread to cast, George," Preacher Mann suggested.

"What are you talking about, Tom?" the county nurse asked.

"Generous George is permitting you to pick out new furniture for each room, paying for it, and adding it to the total lease-purchase price. If we move, we can leave it or pay for it and take it with us," the preacher reported.

"Oh, Mr. Hickman, you truly *are* a very generous person," Nurse Mann said as she hugged the banker.

"I thought I'd never live long enough to hear anyone call George Hickman generous," Finis Lawrence announced.

"Well, let's just keep that a secret. If that gets out to the public, it'll forever damage my reputation as a cruel, heartless banker," George Hickman said.

"He's still a good banker. Part of the deal is we can't move into this fully furnished home until late February. He's using it as a model to sell the next three houses," Preacher Mann reported.

"The man has got to get some benefit for what he's doing. I think it's more than fair. It's much more than fair," the county nurse opined.

"You said we had an appointment with Dr. Whitman at 10:30 am. I'm afraid if we stay and lavish much more praise on Mr. Hickman he may be overcome with emotion," Preacher Mann urged.

"Come on, Generous George, let's get you back before you give away Hickman Bank," Finis Lawrence.

"It's gossip. It's pure gossip. You three have been spending too much time at Jack Wright's store," the banker said as he opened his truck door and started the engine.

After George Hickman and Finis Lawrence drove away, the preacher queried, "Now, what are we doing at Dr. Whitman's office at 10:30 am?"

"Getting test results," Nurse Mann said.

"I didn't realize it was time for your annual tuberculosis test for your job," Preacher Mann remarked.

"It's the results of my pregnancy test," the county nurse responded.

"I didn't know we were trying to get pregnant," the preacher said.

"Well, apparently we weren't trying *not* to get pregnant," Nurse Mann said.

"Indeed," Preacher Mann said under his breath.

*      *      *

When the couple arrived at Smith's Apothecary there were two county sheriff's cars parked outside. Deputy Tom Kelly was stationed outside the drugstore entrance armed with a shotgun and with his service pistol.

"Has there been a robbery?" Preacher Mann said with a chuckle.

"Double shooting. Sheriff Hankins sent me to fetch you, but you weren't at Community Church, Discount Grocery, or Miss Rosie's Bed & Breakfast," the deputy reported.

"He didn't do it. I was with him the whole morning," Nurse Mann replied.

Deputy Kelly neither commented nor smiled at the county nurse's attempt at humor. He simply opened the establishment's door and motioned for them to go inside.

"Preacher take off your preacher's hat and put on your municipal judge's hat. We've got a couple of problems," Sheriff Hankins announced.

"I thought we agreed I would be the city judge until the Mountain Music & Art Festival concluded," the preacher said.

"You agreed to be the city judge until we could find a replacement. It sort of fell through the cracks so you're still on the hook for this situation," Sheriff Hankins reported.

"What's the situation?" Preacher Mann asked.

"Odell Jackson and Willie Long drew shotguns on each other and started shooting. They had a regular gunfight on Highway 70, between Hickman Bank and Discount Grocery," the sheriff explained.

"What in the world caused that exchange?" Nurse Mann asked with a surprised look.

"The Jacksons and the Longs have had a feud since just after the Civil War. It flares up occasionally, but it's generally been just verbal threats and insults. We haven't had anything physical since Odell and Willie were kids," Sheriff Hankins responded.

"Are they seriously injured?" Nurse Mann queried.

"They both took a few buckshot pellets. They were too far from each other to do any real damage. Dr. Whitman has patched them up, but I've got them in custody until I could consult with the city judge," the sheriff replied.

"What caused this altercation?" Preacher Mann asked.

"Neither of the boys will say," Sheriff Hankins said.

"What do you want me to do?" the preacher inquired.

"Hold a hearing. Set bail. Set a trial date. You're the city judge. I'm just the local sheriff. I charged them with a misdemeanor assault and unlawful discharge of a firearm in the city," the sheriff responded.

"Let's hold a preliminary hearing right here, right now," Preacher Mann instructed.

"Is that okay with you, Joe?" Sheriff Hankins inquired of Joe Scott.

"Give me time to call Louis Barrett and set up the room," Joe Scott said.

"Why would he call Louis Barrett?" Nurse Mann queried.

"Free publicity is generally good for business," Preacher Mann suggested.

In less than ten minutes, Louis Barrett arrived, followed by Jack Wright. It was the first-ever municipal court session held in Ferguson. Jack Wright even closed Discount Grocery until the hearing was concluded.

Deputy Kelly brought the two men from Dr. Whitman's clinic to the makeshift courtroom in the apothecary. They were dressed in overalls but without the benefit of their shirts.

Their upper body and face resembled two kids suffering from the measles. The buckshot marks were small, but Dr. Whitman's use of iodine made them quite noticeable.

Preacher Mann was in the apothecary storeroom waiting for those attending the hearing to be seated. Joe Scott cracked open the storeroom door to speak to the preacher.

"What do I say? What do I do? I want to get this right. It's making the front page of The Mountain Gazette this week," Joe Scott said quickly and excitedly.

"All rise. This session of the Ferguson Municipal Court is in session. The Honorable Thomas P. Mann is presiding. Be seated," the preacher instructed.

"Let me get a pad and write it down. I don't want to say it wrong," Joe Scott said, as he hurried to the counter to get pencil and pad.

After everyone was seated, Judge Mann said, "This is the case of the city of Ferguson versus Odell Jackson and Willie Long. We are holding a hearing to test the sufficiency of the sheriff's case and set bail, if necessary."

Before anything else could be said, Odell Jackson exclaimed, "He shot at me and I shot back."

"That's a lie. He came out of Discount Grocery, saw me, and fired his old squirrel gun at me," Willie Long said.

"You two keep quiet. You've both just confessed to criminal acts. You have the right to remain silent and require the sheriff to establish a cause to justify charging you with a crime. Don't make his work any easier," Judge Mann instructed.

"What evidence do you have to offer, Sheriff Hankins, to establish a reason for charging these two men?" Judge Mann inquired.

"Deputy Kelly can tell you what he saw. I think that'll be good enough," the sheriff opined.

After being sworn, Deputy Thomas Kelly took a seat and looked directly at Judge Mann. He was serious-minded in the matter.

"What, if anything, can you tell the court about the events that give rise to the charges against these two men?" the city judge inquired.

"I was driving past Discount Grocery when Odell Jackson raised his gun. I looked in the direction when he pointed his gun and Willie Long had his shotgun raised, too. It wasn't but a few seconds until they both fired. I stopped the patrol car, handcuffed them, and brought them to Dr. Whitman's office," Tom Kelly explained.

"Were they injured?" the city judge asked.

"Looked like they both had been robbing honey from a beehive and got a lot of stings," Deputy Kelly said as the audience chuckled.

Judge Mann looked at the defendants. They cast their eyes toward the floor and didn't make eye contact.

"Gentlemen, it is not required you say anything in your defense. In fact, you are not even required to say anything at trial. The city is required to prove its case against you beyond a reasonable doubt and to a moral certainty. Nevertheless, if you are released today and ordered to return at a future date for trial, will you return?" Judge Mann inquired.

"I'll be here. But Odell Jackson will have a double load of buckshot in his ass before the trial date," Willie Long remarked.

"He'll show up standing up and asking for a new date so Dr. Whitman can pick a double load of buckshot out of his ass," Odell Jackson promised.

"What has caused so much trouble between you two?" Judge Mann asked.

"My daddy told me if I ever got a chance to smoke a Jackson, I had to do it," Willie Long said.

"My daddy told me the same about the Longs. I'm obliged to follow his instructions," Odell Jackson reported.

"What caused them to give you those instructions?" the city judge asked.

"His daddy told him the same thing when he was young," Odell Jackson replied.

"My granddad told my dad the same thing, too," Willie Long said.

"Are your granddads alive?" the municipal judge inquired.

The two young men said in unison, "Yes sir."

"Bail is set at four dollars each for each defendant. Trial is set for January 4th," the city judge said.

"May I speak?" Sheriff Hankins asked.

"Speak your mind, sheriff," the city judge said.

"They'll never be able to make bail. They'll be in jail through the holidays," the sheriff pleaded.

"They should have thought about that before they opted for a gun battle on the streets of Ferguson. I suggest Deputy Kelly get them out of my presence before I set the bail higher," Judge Mann said harshly.

"Is there anything else?" Sheriff Hankins said curtly.

"Do you know the identities of the two grandfathers?" the municipal judge asked.

"It's Frank Long and John Jackson. They're both in their late seventies," Sheriff Hankins reported.

"I'm issuing a warrant for their arrest for conspiracy to engage in a duel. Go pick them up and bring them in. We'll set their hearing as soon as they are in custody," Judge Mann said.

"You want me to go arrest two old men?" Sheriff Hankins asked with incredulity.

"I want you to go arrest two old men for inciting their families to engage in duels on sight and regardless of the location. They are lucky that these are only misdemeanor warrants," Judge Mann said tersely.

"Court is adjourned," Judge Mann said as he stood.

Deputy Kelly took custody of young Jackson and Long and took them to the county jail. Sheriff Hankins stormed out the door to round up the two conspirators. The crowd dispersed.

"I don't like it when you're a city judge," Jack Wright said.

"If that's so, I recommend that the city of Ferguson quickly find a permanent municipal judge and release the temporary one.

"Tom, I think you were harsh. I'm not sure I like you wearing a judge's hat," Nurse Mann remarked.

"For the present, the Lord is our advocate. According to the Apostle Paul eventually, 'we must all appear before the judgment seat of Christ . . .

according to that he hath done, whether it be good or bad.'"

You've seen me serve as an advocate several times. Today you saw me serve as a judge," Preacher Mann replied.

"Indeed," Nurse Mann said pondering the role of advocate and judge.

"I'm back to husband, now. Let's see what Dr. Whitman has to say. I may be taking on the role of father, Preacher Mann said.

As the couple entered the clinic, Dr. Marcus Whitman was giddy about how the preacher had presided over the Jackson-Long case. He was absolutely beaming.

"Preacher, I always knew your callings in life were sometimes a lawyer and most of the time a preacher. Today I know you also have a God-given talent as a judge," the physician remarked.

"You had better be glad I was your advocate in front of the medical board rather than a judge. I would have fried your ass," Preacher Mann remarked.

"We need to find a permanent city judge quickly," Nurse Mann suggested.

"No doubt," the doctor said with raised eyebrows.

"What's the verdict on the pregnancy?" the preacher inquired.

"You didn't waste any time," Dr. Whitman said.

"What do you mean?" Nurse Mann queried.

"The preacher got engaged last Christmas. He got married in April. He'll be a father of twins by late March or early April next year," Dr. Whitman reported.

"It's *twins*! Oh my!" Nurse Mann said as she took a seat.

"How can you tell it's twins?" Preacher Mann asked.

"I heard two heartbeats during the examination. The pregnancy test was a mere formality," the physician said.

"She doesn't look pregnant," the preacher remarked as he looked carefully at the county nurse.

"I can assure you she's pregnant. In fact, she's between four and five months pregnant. She's thin but she'll obviously look pregnant by the time Santa arrives," the doctor chuckled.

"Merry Christmas!" Preacher Mann exclaimed.

"You shouldn't be looking for three wise men from the east," Nurse Mann said giving the preacher a stern look.

"No, it was just a preacher from the south," Dr. Whitman remarked.

"And Wheaties, the breakfast of champions," Nurse Mann added.

*   *   *

By the time the couple had finished their business with Dr. Whitman, Sheriff Hankins arrived with a handcuffed Frank Long and John Jackson. The two men were elderly, and it was a chore for them to make it from the sheriff's patrol car to the makeshift courtroom in Scott's Apothecary.

"Here are your two conspirators, judge," Sheriff Hankins reported.

"Why did you two men tell your sons to shoot Jacksons and Longs on sight?" Judge Mann asked.

"That's what my daddy told me," John Jackson replied.

"Mine, too," Frank Long added.

"What started the original feud over 75 years ago?" Judge Mann asked.

"My daddy never said. He just told me we were feuding with the Longs, and if I had the chance, to shoot one on sight," John Jackson said.

"My daddy told me the same thing. He said we were feuding with the Jacksons and shoot them on sight," the elder Long reported.

"Did any Longs ever shoot any Jacksons or vice versa?" Judge Mann asked.

"Not until today. It was a double," Frank Long said.

"It took about 75 years," John Jackson added.

"I think I need to release your two grandsons for following the instructions of their patriarchs, something like the English law of coverture where a wife must obey her husband, or a servant must obey his master, and put you two in jail for a year each," the judge opined.

"Can't you do something less drastic, judge? These are good men from good families," Sheriff Hankins pleaded.

"I'm not sure about that. They've taught their grandchildren to have gun battles in public, kill each other's families on sight, and risk death or serious injury to innocent members of the public. If someone had been killed, I'd be charging them with murder and likely hanging them," the municipal judge threatened.

"Judge Mann, can I please talk to you in private?" Sheriff Hankins inquired.

Judge Mann made his way to the apothecary storeroom. Sheriff Hankins followed closely. When they reached the storeroom, Sheriff Hankins closed the door behind him.

"Preacher, I'm begging you to show a little mercy on these two families. You're acting like a tyrant. We need more mercy and less justice," Sheriff Hankins pleaded.

"Did you send for young Long and Jackson?" he inquired.

The preacher motioned for the Sheriff to open the storeroom door. Both men returned to the makeshift courtroom area.

"At the insistence of Sheriff Hankins, I'm going to offer you men a way to avoid jail for both of you and your grandsons," the city judge said.

"Say on," both men replied in unison.

"I'm going to release the two young men because they were following your instructions. There were no serious injuries and they have no prior convictions. Their cases are dismissed.

I'll follow Tennessee law and permit a one-year pre-trial diversion. If you two instruct your families that this feud is over, there are no further altercations between the Jacksons and the Longs, and you remain problem-free until next Thanksgiving, your cases will disappear. It'll be like this never happened," Judge Mann said.

"You'll have no problems with the Longs," Frank Long said.

"There won't be any difficulties with the Jacksons either," John Jackson said.

"Based on your recommendation, and the promises of the two gentlemen, this case is diverted. They are free to go," the municipal judge said.

"Much obliged," Frank Long said.

"We won't let you down," John Jackson said.

"I consider that a miracle, Tom," Nurse Mann remarked.

"It's two miracles in one day:  The stories of Generous George Hickman and Caring Clarence Hankins," Preacher Mann opined.

"It's actually three miracles in a day," Dr. Marcus Whitman remarked.

"What's the other one?" Preacher Mann queried.

"It's Generous George, Caring Clarence, and Prolific Preacher," the physician responded.

"Louis Barrett will definitely write a story about the prolific preacher," the county nurse said.

"No doubt," Preacher Mann said with a huge sigh.

# 7. Innocence Violated

A light snowfall covered Ferguson's buildings, homes, and highways overnight. Smoke rose from chimneys and the morning sun caused a bright glare covering the landscape. It also caused the newly fallen snow to melt quickly.

Because of its location high on the Cumberland Plateau, coupled with attendance by many older members, Community Church started its Sunday services at noon on snowy Sundays and dismissed the evening services. Today was no exception.

Josh Sullivan finished the Sunday school lesson, the opening song, service, and prayer concluded, and Preacher Mann had completed about half his post-Christmas sermon entitled, 'The Dark Side of the Nativity.' It was the gospel narrative about Herod's slaughter of all male infants under two years of age in Bethlehem in hopes of killing Jesus.

Preacher Mann would eventually write in his journal that both the gospel narrative and the events of December 7, 1941, were times when innocence was violated.

Jeremy Ford rushed through the front door at Community Church and displayed a rather frantic look. He pointed to himself and then to the preacher. He indicated it was very important that he immediately speak to the preacher.

The two men conversed while Preacher Mann nodded at what Jeremy was saying. The congregation waited for an announcement that was almost certain to be bad news.

"Jeremy Ford serves as a civilian communications analyst for the U.S. military. While performing his duties this morning, he learned that at 7:53 am Hawaiian time, or about an hour ago local time, Japanese naval and air forces attacked our naval and air stations in Honolulu, Hawaii. Hickam Field was also attacked. It seems there has been considerable loss of life, Preacher Mann announced to the disbelief, sobs, and grief exhibited by the church members.

Community Church held a closing prayer and services were dismissed for the congregants to return to their homes to listen for further news. Jeremy brought a large radio with additional large speakers for those who wanted to stay at the meetinghouse and listen to news reports.

Preacher Mann stood at the front door to thank each member for attending services. In many instances, he was tasked with consoling and encouraging the attendees.

When the crowd had cleared, Jack Wright said, "Don't worry preacher. We're going to win this war."

"There are no winners in war, only survivors," Preacher Mann opined.

The following day President Franklin D. Roosevelt addressed Congress and called for a Declaration of War against Japan and the Axis powers. In less than an hour, the War Resolution passed, declaring a state of war had existed since the Pearl Harbor attack the previous day.

Ferguson, the United States, and the world would be forever changed by World War II. Veterans of the Great War, or World War I, knew it all too well.

By mid-week several of the young men in the area had volunteered for military service. The Mountain Gazette followed the story closely, and much of the citizenry was concerned about the country's preparedness for a long and bloody conflict.

Preacher Mann spent much of his time counseling and consoling members and non-members alike during the days following the attack on Pearl Harbor.

Rationing began quickly with restrictions on gasoline purchases. It was eventually extended to other areas such as bacon, sugar, butter, tires, and even shoes.

A national speed limit of 35 miles per hour was enacted. Its purpose was to save gasoline and tires.

Automobile racing was banned. All tires in excess of five per driver were confiscated by the government.

Within two years rationing was extended to typewriters, silk, nylon, fuel oil, and stoves. Meat, lard, shortening and food oils, cheese, processed foods, dried fruits, coal, and jams and jellies were added to the list.

Due to factories retooling from consumer goods to war production, many things were in short supply. The scarcity of penicillin caused a triage panel at each hospital to determine which patient would receive the drug.

Ration books were eventually printed in mass. Both retailers and citizens were expected to follow the rules. Black marketing, or buying and selling outside the system, was criminally prosecuted.

"I haven't seen you in a few days," Jack Wright remarked as Preacher Mann entered the store.

"How's business?" the preacher asked.

"Business would be good if I had anything to sell and didn't have to deal with ration coupons that are being printed," the merchant exclaimed.

"It's gotten that strict already?" Preacher Mann asked.

"I can't get anything from the wholesalers because they all know what's coming. They're selling to black marketers before it becomes strictly illegal. I bet

Henry Wooden has made more money this week than he made all of last year," Jack Wright reported.

"It won't be long until rationing causes that carousel to stop. Henry will be moanin' the blues," the preacher said with a chuckle.

A car pulled up in front of Discount Grocery. An older gentleman walked into the store. He held two telegram envelopes in his hand.

"I've got two telegrams for April Dalton. I'm told she is the mother of Josh and Jake Dalton," the courier explained.

"She lives on Brotherton Mountain in a cabin near Miller's Lake. There's no phone. It'd be hard to get up there this time of year," Jack Wright said.

"I really need to get these telegrams to her. They're official, and from the U.S. Army," the older gentleman explained.

"I know the family. The father died a few months ago and Miss April is illiterate," Preacher Mann explained.

"Illegitimate? That's no concern of mine. I just need to give her the telegrams," the courier remarked.

"The preacher is saying she can't read and write," Jack Wright explained.

"Can you get these envelopes to her? I can leave them with a preacher," the old man said.

"Do you know what's in them?" Preacher Mann said.

"Not a word," the courier replied.

"I'd have to explain what's in them. That means I'd have to open them and read them," Preacher Mann said.

"You do whatever you need to do preacher. I'm on my way to Crab Orchard in Cumberland County. I need to get there and get back to Cookeville before dark," the courier explained, as he handed the envelopes to the preacher.

After the courier left, Jack Wright remarked, "I haven't seen those Dalton boys in these parts for over two years. I wonder whatever happened to them."

"They spent two years at the Civilian Conservation Corps camp in Corbin, Kentucky, were honorably discharged, and then they both joined the U.S. Army," Preacher Mann reported.

"How do you know that?" the merchant inquired.

"I got a letter from the camp commander commending them and announcing their enlistment. I knew Lieutenant Colonel Cameron Shipman from my time in the war," the preacher answered.

"Are you going to open those envelopes?" the storekeeper asked.

Louis Barrett walked into Discount Grocery just as Jack Wright asked the question to the preacher. His interest piqued when he saw the envelopes were marked Western Union.

"Who's getting telegrams in Ferguson?" Louis Barrett asked.

"They're for Jake and Josh Dalton's mother, April Dalton," Jack Wright announced.

"I see I need to do a refresher sermon on gossiping," Preacher Mann said with a snarl.

"If the content of those envelopes happens to be what I think it is, it may be quite newsworthy," Louis Barrett suggested.

"What do you think is in the envelopes?" the preacher queried.

"Those are draft notices for Jake and Josh Dalton. They're the right age," the newspaper editor opined.

"It can't be. They're already in the U.S. Army," Jack Wright replied.

The preacher gave the merchant a very stern look and placed his right index finger vertically across his lips. It was an overt signal for the merchant to hush.

"Preacher, you know something you are not telling us," Louis Barrett opined.

"Drive me up to Brotherton Mountain. If Miss April wants you to know, she can tell you. Otherwise, we'll be letting the mystery be," Preacher Mann responded.

"That's fair enough. Let's go to Brotherton Mountain," Louis Barrett offered.

"Can I go, too?" Jack Wright asked.

"No!" Preacher Mann said firmly, as the pair made their way to the front door of Discount Grocery.

*     *     *

It was about a twenty-minute drive from Discount Grocery to the Dalton cabin atop Brotherton Mountain. The preacher did not speak, and the newspaperman respected his period of concentration and reflection.

Preacher Mann knocked on the cabin door and announced, "Miss April, it's the preacher. I need to see you."

"I ain't been selling any of that moonshine. I've been buying a jug along to help with my rheumatism. I drink a cup and I'm able to sleep all night," Miss April said as she opened the screen door and motioned for the men to come inside.

"This is Louis Barrett. He's the editor of the local newspaper. He's also a deacon at Community Church. Today he's a deacon and not a newspaperman," Preacher Mann explained.

"I don't think an old woman taking a cup of moonshine whiskey is any big news anyway – especially if she's a widow woman," Miss April said with a chuckle.

"I've got two telegrams from the U.S. Army about your sons, Jake and Josh," Preacher Mann said.

"Are they in trouble? What do those things say?" April Dalton inquired.

"I haven't opened them, Miss April. I need your permission to read them and explain them to you," the preacher explained.

"I can't read. I'd be obliged if you opened them. It's alright if Deacon Barrett hears too," the old woman said.

Preacher Mann opened both envelopes and read each telegram carefully. He cleared his throat and looked directly at the Dalton boys' mother.

"Miss April, Jake and Josh were stationed at Hickam Field in Honolulu, Hawaii. They were both killed in action as a result of the Japanese attack this past Sunday. I am so very sorry," Preacher Mann said.

"Does it say they'll be sending their bodies back home?" the old woman asked tearfully.

"It doesn't say. But after being in the army myself during the last war, I am almost certain they'll be buried in Hawaii, and their personal effects will eventually be sent to you," the preacher explained.

"That's an awfully pretty place. I got postcards from them a few months ago," Miss April said as she opened a small chest on the dining table before returning with some items in her hands.

"Here are four picture cards they sent me," she explained.

"It's like paradise," Louis Barrett said as he was handed the cards by the preacher.

"The Lord told that thief on the cross he'd be with him in paradise. I have little doubt that's where my two boys are right now," Miss April opined.

"I haven't any doubt about that either," Preacher Mann replied.

"Preacher, when Josh and Jake got their first haircuts, I cut off a lock of their hair and saved it. It's all I got of them. I want you to give them a proper funeral and bury these," Miss April implored.

"I would be honored," Preacher Mann nodded and said.

"Miss April, Josh and Jake Dalton are truly heroes. Their deaths should be reported in The Mountain Gazette," Louis Barrett suggested.

"Well, their father used to say, 'Those boys are too mean for heaven and too good for hell' People around here need to know that they gave their lives for this country," Miss April said.

"I recommend the funeral and burial take place at Community Church. We will put up a grave marker that commemorates them. We can leave space for any others that are sacrificed in this war," Preacher Mann offered.

"I've got no money for that," Miss April said with a slight smile.

"Don't worry. The church will take care of that," Preacher Mann remarked.

"No, the city of Ferguson will take care of the expenses related to the grave marker and the war memorial," Louis Barrett countered.

"I'd be powerful obliged," the Dalton boys' mother said tearfully.

* * *

Louis Barrett reported about the heroic deaths of Josh and Jake Dalton in The Mountain Gazette. He even published an extra edition.

He told Jack Wright, who mentioned it in his journal, that the newspaperman said he was glad he was seated when Preacher Mann reported their deaths to their mother. He told Jack Wright he fought back tears as their widowed mother offered the locks of their hair for burial.

The Mountain Gazette carried the text of Preacher Mann's funeral sermon for Jake and Josh Dalton. There were over five hundred attendees. The crowd was so large the preacher gave his sermon from the tall porch of Discount Grocery, across the road from Community Church.

An excerpt of Preacher Mann's sermon as recorded in The Mountain Gazette article read:

"An old gospel song says 'My Lord Keeps Record.' It tells us in pertinent part:

"Now I want to be doing the will of my Lord
As I travel this wearisome land
So I won't be ashamed of my record up there
When I stand at my Savior's right hand

My Lord keeps a record
Of the moments I'm living down here
Yes, he knows all about me
All my troubles, my sorrows, and fear."

When Josh and Jake Dalton left mortality, their sacrifice became an immortal record of their love and sacrifice for all of us.

Near the end of his days, the great Apostle Paul wrote, 'I have fought a good fight. I have finished my course, I have kept the faith: Henceforth, there is laid up for me a crown of righteousness, which the Lord, the righteous judge shall give me at that day.'

These two young men fought a good fight. They too finished their course. They kept the faith. We can rest assured their record will have the Lord granting them their crowns. Amen."

Editor's Note: Eventually World War II ended. There were sixty-eight war deaths of citizens from Putnam County, Tennessee. It is our task to never forget their sacrifice upon the altar of freedom.

# 8. Patriots

It was a warm but blustery, early March day that had the preacher waiting to order his Friday lunch at the Bluebird Café. It was the one day of the workweek that caused Preacher Mann to enjoy an extended noonday meal. It gave him the opportunity to attend the practice session for WNOX-AM's Friday Night Frolics.

"Come in, preacher. You can sit at my table," Dr. Marcus Whitman invited.

"Does that mean you're buying my lunch?" the preacher asked with a smile.

"I'll even buy you a piece of that seven-layer chocolate cake Ruth Bell bakes, too," the physician offered.

"My wife has me on diet. It's doesn't include Miss Ruth's chocolate cake," Preacher Mann explained.

"Like you tell Jack Wright: I won't tell anyone, and I won't even ask anyone if they know about it," the doctor promised.

"If I get caught, you'll be in as much trouble as I will," Preacher Mann said with a chuckle.

"Is the good doctor buying our lunch today?" Jack Wright asked as he entered the Bluebird and walked toward Dr. Whitman's table.

"He's even buying dessert, too," Preacher Mann reported.

"What's the occasion?" the merchant inquired.

"Anna Mae is in Cookeville running errands for Joe Scott. I have no appointments this afternoon. The clinic is closed except for emergencies. I decided to listen to the Friday Frolics practice session," Dr. Whitman explained.

"I hear he's turning from general practitioner to pediatrician," the storekeeper said.

"That's right. He's got the Barrett baby, the Kelly baby, and his own baby, all born in the last week," Preacher Mann acknowledged.

"You are within a month of Nurse Mann birthing twins," Dr. Whitman said with a chuckle.

"There's Cecil Smith. I'll get him over here and we can find out who's on the show tonight," Jack Wright remarked.

Cecil Smith approached the table and said, "Sorry, gents. Doris will be out to get your order in a few minutes. We'll be ready to go as soon as our guest musician gets here from Miss Rosie's."

"Who's tonight's special guest?" Jack Wright inquired.

"It's a young fellow from Montgomery, Alabama. Coleman Walker said he appears regularly on WSFA-AM there. He's making a tour of several radio shows. He hopes to get on WSM's Grand Ole Opry, too," Cecil Smith responded.

"What type of music does he play?" Preacher Mann queried.

"He mostly performs country, honky-tonk, and some gospel. Hank Williams is really good. He's only eighteen, but he sounds older," Cecil Smith said.

Dr. Whitman interrupted the conversation, pointed toward the door, and said, "Looks like you've got a couple of 'shiners wanting to talk to you, preacher."

Before Preacher Mann could leave his seat and make his way to the door, John Lee Pettimore and Tim Huddleston stood at the table and nodded.

"We need to talk some extract business," John Lee Pettimore announced.

"I believe you know both Dr. Marcus Whitman, the town doctor, and Jack Wright, the owner of Discount Grocery," Preacher Mann remarked.

All four men acknowledged they were acquainted. Before the conversation could continue, Doris Smith appeared at the table with her order book.

"It's chicken and dumplings today, gentlemen. We have no ground beef for meatloaf. We have no fresh or cured pork. It's chicken and dumplings or a four-vegetable plate," she reported.

"Did we get here too late?" Preacher Mann asked.

"It's shortages due to rationing. It's just not available from the wholesalers," Doris Smith lamented.

"John Lee, does any of your family or friends have slabs of bacon or hams to sell?" Preacher Mann queried.

"We've got plenty. We can get some fresh pork and sell a side of beef, too," Mr. Pettimore reported.

"When you get ready, come out to the kitchen. I'll feed you all you can hold, and we'll work a deal on some bacon, ham, fresh pork, and fresh beef," Doris promised.

"Preacher, we can't get sugar and yeast. Without sugar and yeast, there's no alcohol for extract. It's that simple," Tim Huddleston said bluntly.

"What can you do?" Preacher Mann asked of Jack Wright.

"I've been getting them all the gray market sugar I can get my hands on. But they use a lot of sugar," the merchant replied.

"What's gray market sugar?" Dr. Whitman inquired.

"If there are things that are rationed, but a family doesn't need them, for example, tires, I'll take their tire ration coupons and trade them to Henry Wooden for sugar. I give the family a partial credit for the tires," the merchant explained.

"Is that legal?" Dr. Whitman asked Preacher Mann. "He's supposed to see a family tear the coupon from the ration book. But if a family just presents a couple of coupons that have been torn out by mistake, inadvertence, or excusable neglect, he can accept it," Preacher Mann said.

"What about trading ration coupons?" Dr. Whitman pressed.

"It won't be a problem unless there's an extensive audit. He had better keep good records," the preacher said with a chuckle.

"What's the best way to help them with their yeast and sugar dilemma?" Dr. Whitman queried.

"Henry Wooden is the wholesaler that buys every bottle of extract from Joe Scott. I recommend John Lee and Tim go to Joe Scott's and set up an immediate meeting with Henry Wooden.

Also, I recommend Jack Wright make plans to be present. Henry will probably be able to get the yeast and sugar in quantity, but it is best that it is not purely black market, or sold outside the rationing system," Preacher Mann remarked.

"Are you going to be there, too?" Jack Wright inquired.

"If necessary, but I think this is more of a bookkeeping problem than a supply problem. Now Doris Smith has a supply problem," Preacher Mann said with a slight chuckle.

"We're taking care of Miss Doris' supply problem today. You'll be eating country ham by breakfast tomorrow, preacher," John Lee Pettimore promised.

Doris returned to the table with three chicken and dumpling specials for Dr. Marcus Whitman, Jack Wright, and Preacher Mann. There was no scarcity of chicken, dumplings, pinto beans or turnip greens on the plates.

"I bring yours next," Doris said to John Lee Pettimore and Tim Huddleston.

"If it's the same to you, ma'am, we'll take our meal and talk business in the kitchen," Mr. Pettimore said.

"Follow me. It's all you can eat," Doris Smith promised.

While they were eating lunch, a tall, thin, young man in a cowboy hat, boots, and a western-style suit, carrying a Martin guitar, entered the Bluebird and walked toward the small stage in the dining area. It was obviously the young man Cecil Smith had talked about.

It wasn't long before Cecil Smith and the young man approached Dr. Whitman's table. They were all three introduced to Hiram King Williams.

"My friends call me Hank," young Williams said with a smile.

"He's performing at least two original songs on the show tonight: a country song called, 'Move It on

Over' and a gospel song called, 'Wealth Won't Save Your Soul,'" Cecil Smith reported.

"Which one do you want to hear for my practice song?" Hank Williams asked.

"I vote for 'Move It on Over,'" Preacher Mann replied, with Jack Wright and Dr. Marcus Whitman giving nods of approval.

Hank took the stage along with the Smith Brothers. His strong, tenor voice was unique and strong. He crooned with the Smith Brothers as backup singers:

> **"Came in last night at half-past ten**
> **That baby of mine wouldn't let me in**
> **So move it on over (move it on over)**
> **Move it on over (move it on over)**
> **Move over little dog**
> **'Cause the big dog's moving in."**

While young Williams continued to sing, the trio finished their meals and Doris cleared away their lunch plates. Like clockwork, she brought Preacher Mann a large slice of the seven-layer dark chocolate cake.

Jack Wright pointed to the slice of chocolate cake and then to himself. When Doris made eye contact with Dr. Whitman, he shook his head and held up his hand indicating he wasn't having dessert.

Before Preacher Mann could pick up a fork and make any headway on the chocolate cake, his wife appeared beside the table. Both Dr. Whitman and Jack Wright held their breath until she spoke.

"Tom, surely you haven't gone off your diet and are eating that huge slab of chocolate cake?" Nurse Mann inquired.

"That one's for Dr. Whitman. Doris is bringing Jack Wright's piece of cake next," Preacher Mann replied.

Dr. Whitman picked up the dessert fork and took a big bite of the chocolate cake while everyone watched.

"You should have had a slice of this cake. It is delicious," Dr. Whitman remarked.

"Tom, we need to take time to see Finis Lawrence. He's already a week late on finishing our house and it appears nothing has been done on any of those houses all week long," Nurse Mann reported.

"Leave your car here and we'll take my truck. I need to have a brief word or two with Dr. Whitman and Jack Wright. It won't take but a couple of minutes," Preacher Mann promised.

"I'll meet you at the car," the county nurse said with a smile and a wink.

"Whew! You were one bite away from judgment day," Dr. Whitman remarked.

"He's living life on the edge if he gets her stirred up," Jack Wright opined.

"Nunc pro tunc," the preacher responded.

"What's he saying?" Jack Wright inquired.

"It's Latin for 'now for then,'" Dr. Whitman instructed.

"What does that mean?" Jack Wright asked with interest.

"It essentially means 'that which was done should have retroactively been done,'" Dr. Whitman explained.

"I get it. He should have left that cake alone when he ordered it," Jack Wright chuckled.

"Indeed," Preacher Mann responded.

Nurse Mann opened the door of the Bluebird Café and announced, "Tom, I'm waiting."

Preacher Mann responded as he stood and turned toward the door, "On my way, dear."

Once the preacher exited the café, Jack Wright said, "I knew it would happen, but I'm surprised it was this quick."

"Sooner or later, it happens to all of us," Dr. Whitman said with a big sigh and continued to eat the huge slice of chocolate cake.

*   *   *

When Preacher Mann and his wife arrived at Martin Sawmill & Salvage, Finis Martin immediately knew he was about to face judgment day himself. He wasn't looking forward to the next few minutes.

"Finis Martin, you were a week late in getting that house finished and you haven't made any progress

115

this week. Now George Hickman will be wanting at least two weeks to show the house before we get possession," Nurse Mann said indignantly.

"Well . . . er . . . I mean . . . it is like," Finis Martin stammered before being interrupted by Nurse Mann.

"I'm due to deliver these twins in about a month or so. The last thing I need is to be boarding two crying infants at Miss Rosie's Bed & Breakfast," Nurse Mann said as her voice became louder.

"Beth, I think we should hear what Finis Martin has to say before you start the tar and feathering of the man," Preacher Mann suggested.

"I don't have the workers. After the Pearl Harbor attack, a lot of my workers volunteered for military service. Now I'm starting to lose skilled tradesmen to the military base at Oak Ridge. Additionally, the draft has been instituted and I'll lose more. I've had to put almost everyone on sawmill work to meet my lumber contract with the U.S. Army," Finis Martin explained.

"Have you tried to hire some of the black farmers and black sharecroppers?" Preacher Mann inquired.

"I've put out the word but there are no takers," Finis Martin replied.

"What's their objection?" Nurse Mann inquired.

"It's the Lee Bell syndrome," Finis Martin said.

"What's that?" the county nurse asked.

"He pays white workers more than black workers for the same job. If he levels the pay, he will likely lose a portion of his white workers," Preacher Mann replied.

"He's exactly right," Finis Martin said.

"Tom, you need to get this handled. We can't put our children in a small, shared room at a bed and breakfast," Nurse Mann said tearfully.

"You're the perfect person to get this resolved, preacher," Finis Martin opined.

"What's George Hickman's position on this?" Preacher Mann queried.

"He sees it as the contractor's problem, not the bank's problem," Finis Martin reported.

"It's starting to become his problem. He's almost a month late on starting the three new homes. It won't be long before he has to deal with SheMammy Martin, one of his largest depositors," Preacher Mann observed.

"Why don't you get Miss Ruth to arrange a meeting with those black men interested in working for Martin Sawmill & Salvage? You can mediate this problem. We need a home for our children," Nurse Mann said with a break in her voice.

"Your boss is a carpenter. I'm sure he'll give you some advice," Finis Martin said with a smile.

"Beth, finish your rounds and I'll go see Miss Ruth at the Bluebird," the preacher said.

"I won't ask about that piece of chocolate cake," Nurse Mann promised.

"What piece of chocolate cake?" the preacher asked indignantly.

"That piece of chocolate cake you'll be eating in the kitchen when you're talking with Miss Ruth Bell," Nurse Mann replied.

*   *   *

Miss Ruth was able to arrange a meeting at her cabin for about a dozen men and the preacher. She said the men were hopeful that the preacher could do something to resolve the situation.

Jim Casey was appointed to be spokesman for the black workers. He was both articulate and logical in his thinking.

"Preacher, it's this simple. Lee Bell was murdered, and you were almost killed helping us get equal pay for our crops. Whites and blacks get the same rate of pay. Race is not an issue," Jim Casey explained.

"So, if I understand you correctly, you won't work beside white workers who are being paid a higher rate for the same work," Preacher Mann said.

"Not if it's only because of race. If he has more skill or has a specialty, that's not a problem. Laboring is laboring. If whites and blacks are paid differently because of the color of their skin, it won't work. It doesn't work in the military. It's the same rank, same pay," Mr. Casey explained.

"Suppose Finis Martin puts his white workers on from 6:00 am till 2:00 pm and his black workers on from 2:00 pm until 10:00. He can have all of you loading rail cars when there's not enough light to safely run the sawmill," Preacher Mann asked.

"We'll do it. That would be fair," Jim Casey said.

"I will make sure that The Mountain Gazette hails you as patriots who are willing to work under hardship to help the war effort," Preacher Mann promised.

"Patriots is a fine name for us," Jim Casey said to the applause of the crowd.

"It's a proper and fitting name. Lee Bell would be proud," the preacher opined.

\*     \*     \*

Preacher Mann took his wife and returned to Martin Sawmill & Salvage early the following day. Finis Martin waited to smile until he noticed the both Preacher Mann and Nurse Mann were smiling.

It was fortuitous that George Hickman was present, too. He was encouraged Nurse Mann appeared to be in a relaxed mood.

"Well, if it can be done, the preacher and the Lord will get it done," George Hickman remarked.

Preacher Mann explained the two-shift option. It resolved the racial issues and did not increase costs to Martin Sawmill or Hickman Bank.

"Now Preacher, we're approaching the three-year mark. I know there's more to this deal than you're telling. I'm waiting to hear how you're going to take away part of our profit. I know you'll be fair, but it's the way you're made," George Hickman explained.

"Here's the balance of the deal: Every worker that starts work with Martin Sawmill, beginning Monday, March 15, 1941, and completes one full month, will be given $25 store credit at Martin Sawmill & Salvage," Preacher Mann said.

George Hickman & Finis Martin looked at each other and then stared at the preacher. They were quite puzzled at the additional requirement.

"We'll do it, preacher. But the credit will be mostly for black workers because you have them starting on Monday. How will we be able to explain it?" Finis Martin queried.

"Call it a patriot credit. These men have left farms and fields to come to the aid of their country. They are working on a critical government materials contract to permit more skilled workers to better apply themselves. It is a one-time credit," Preacher Mann said.

"I like the concept," George Hickman exclaimed.

"What's the Lord's cut?" Finis Martin inquired with a smile.

"Not a cent. It's actually a return from George Hickman's 'casting bread on the water,'" Preacher Mann said.

"You need to write that concept in a book!" Finis Martin suggested.

"Someone already did. It's called the Bible," Preacher Mann replied with a chuckle.

# 9.  The Ides of March

In his play, *Julius Caesar*, William Shakespeare writes that a soothsayer attracts Caesar's attention and tells him, "Beware of the ides of March." In his play, and in reality, Julius Caesar was indeed assassinated on the ides of March, that is, March 15 in the year 44 B.C.

For millennia, going back to ancient traditions and superstitions, the idea that the ides of March is a portent of doom has been ingrained in the human psyche. Any unfortunate event occurring in mid-March was often attributed to the ides of March superstition.

"The ides of March are upon us," Jack Wright remarked as Preacher Mann entered Discount Grocery.

"It appears you have gone from cub reporter to soothsayer," the preacher replied.

"I just heard about it on the radio. It's awful," the merchant responded.

"What is awful?" Preacher Mann inquired.

"A blizzard hit North Dakota and northern Minnesota with little warning, killing 151 people. The temperature dropped twenty degrees in less than 15 minutes with wind reaching 50 miles per hour. They're digging people out of cars who've frozen to death," Jack Wright reported.

"That's terrible," the preacher said.

"Two years ago, Germany invaded Czechoslovakia on the ides of March," the merchant continued.

"And you think those things occurred because of the ides of March curse?" Preacher Mann asked.

"All I'm saying is we should always be circumspect around mid-March," Jack Wright warned.

"I'll keep that in mind," Preacher Mann said as he rolled his eyes.

Shortly thereafter a U.S. Army captain and a sergeant major entered Discount Grocery. The two men looked very familiar to Jack Wright.

"Have you two returned for a rematch?" Preacher Mann said with a huge smile.

"No, sir! We had enough of you last time," the captain said, as he extended his right hand to accept a handshake from the preacher.

"Looks like you two have been promoted twice. You've gone from a second lieutenant to a captain, and the sergeant from a master sergeant to a staff sergeant major. That's impressive," Preacher Mann remarked.

"Your sworn testimony said we bravely and professionally defended our position and then stood down to avoid unnecessary bloodshed of civilians and state militia impressed our commanding officer," Captain John Anderson reported.

"Also, it got us commendations, our first promotion, and reassignment to a new post," Sergeant Major Douglas Richmond added.

"I wasn't aware the Army Corps of Engineers had a facility in this area," the preacher replied.

The captain and sergeant major looked at each other. Neither of them replied to the preacher's remark.

After about a minute of dead silence, the captain reached inside his coat pocket, retrieved a letter, handed it to the preacher, and said, "This will help you understand our situation and why we are here."

Preacher Mann carefully read the letter but occasionally looked at the two uniformed soldiers. When he had finished the letter, he still had a confused look on his face.

"We need to discuss this," Preacher Mann said.

"That communication is for your eyes only. I'm not sure it should be disclosed to anyone else," Captain John Anderson remarked.

"Permit me to introduce you to Mr. Jack Wright. He is the proprietor of this store and one of the deacons at Community Church. I trust him with my life," Preacher Mann replied.

"Mr. Wright, we can step outside and speak with the preacher or stay inside these walls. Anything you learn from this conversation involves national security during wartime. If it is revealed to anyone else, you could be subject to a prison term," Captain Anderson explained.

"Let me close and lock the front door to prevent anyone from walking inside unannounced. Nothing said here will be repeated. I give you my word," Jack Wright promised.

Once the store had been secured, Jack Wright nodded for the preacher to continue. What they were about to hear was beyond shocking.

"Our commanding officer, Major General Leslie Groves, oversees the Clinton Engineering Works located near Knoxville, Tennessee. He is tasked with quickly building a facility for the U.S. Army that includes residential, institutional, and commercial buildings," the captain explained.

"Why does he need my assistance? How does he know of my existence?" Preacher Mann queried.

"General Groves has long been an engineer and senior officer in the Army Corps of Engineers. He became aware of the Cherokee Burial Grounds incident due to a detailed investigatory report submitted to the Chief of Engineers and Secretary of State Cordell Hull," the captain replied.

"More recently he became aware of your handling of the labor dispute at Lawrence Sawmill, which resulted in lumber production being doubled from that location," Sergeant Major Richmond added.

"So now he wants me to recruit Jeremy Ford for a commission with the U.S. Army Signal Corps to be stationed at his facility?" Preacher Mann asked with incredulity.

"He's not able to serve. He had polio and gets around on crutches. He can't pass the physical. He's exempt," Jack Wright opined.

"He's already a civilian employee with the Army Signal Corps and a graduate engineer from Tennessee Polytechnic University. He's been involved with electronics and radio since he was a child. Hell, the receivers that he's built and is using are better than the best equipment available to our military," Captain Anderson explained.

"How do you intend to get him into the military, given his disability?" Preacher Mann asked.

"He'll be processed through the Army Signal Corps, commissioned as a non-flying first lieutenant, and stationed at our facility," the captain explained.

"What will he be doing?" Preacher Mann asked.

"That's classified," the captain responded.

"If I don't know what he'll be doing, how can I ask him to do it?" Preacher Mann replied with exasperation.

"He will be working on a highly classified radio beam location system for spotting planes and ships. That's all *I* even know," Captain Anderson said.

"There's one incentive that may convince him to seriously consider serving his country as a uniformed officer," the sergeant major offered.

"What's that?" Jack Wright inquired.

"Congress suspended all amateur radio operations for the remainder of the war. We are aware young Ford has been passing third party health and welfare messages between certain persons in Europe, and those in the states, by utilizing the amateur radio frequencies. This afternoon, two F.B.I. agents will be in Ferguson to arrest him for violating federal law," Captain John Anderson replied.

"The ides of March," Jack Wright said, looking directly at Preacher Mann.

"Jack, call Jeremy Ford and tell him I need to see him and his parents immediately. Tell them to meet me at Community Church," the preacher instructed.

While Jack Wright made his way to the wall-mounted telephone, Preacher Mann said, "It'll take about twenty to thirty minutes for them to get here. I recommend you get a soda at Scott's Apothecary. Be at the meetinghouse across the road in a half-hour."

The captain and the sergeant major nodded affirmatively and made their way to the front door of the store and entered their army staff car. Jack Wright returned and nodded affirmatively that the message had been delivered.

"Beware of the ides of March! That's what I said," Jack Wright exclaimed.

"It might have been better if you hadn't waited till the very day," Preacher Mann said with a derisive look.

Before Jack Wright could reply, two men in black suits arrived at Discount Grocery. They announced they were looking for Thomas 'Raven' Mann.

"I'm Preacher Mann. How can I help you?" the preacher replied.

"Gary Simpkins said you could help us locate a young man by the name of Jeremy Ford," one of the agents responded.

"It depends on why you need him," Preacher Mann remarked.

"It's official government business. It's none of your concern," the other agent replied with a smirk.

"Then you and Whitehorse can officially kiss my ass," the preacher said belligerently.

"We might just arrest your ass for obstruction of justice," the first agent said smugly.

"And I might just file suit under 42 U.S.C. 1983 and 42 U.S.C. 1985 and settle for your termination in lieu of monetary damages, gentlemen. I recommend you keep your mouths shut until you talk to your supervisor, Gary Simpkins," Preacher Mann said indignantly.

"The phone's back there. I donate the cost of the call," Jack Wright said with a chuckle.

"He wants to talk to you," the second F.B.I. agent reported.

When Preacher Mann picked up the phone and announced his presence, Agent Simpkins said, "I can't believe you suggested two of my best agents kiss your ass."

"If these two are your best, you are scraping the bottom of the barrel. I told them to tell you that *you* could kiss my ass, too," Preacher Mann said as he increased the volume of his voice.

"Look, they're up there investigating a claim that a civilian employee of the Army Signal Corps, Jeremy Ford, has been making illegal amateur radio contacts with European stations. They just need to speak with him at this point," Gary Simpkins explained.

"They can't speak with him," Preacher Mann said firmly.

"What do you mean they can't speak with him?" Gary Simpkins replied in astonishment.

"I represent him. He's not talking to the F.B.I. – ever," Preacher Mann said decisively.

"I'll instruct them to take him into custody," Gary Simpkins replied.

"They had better have an indictment or a presentment in their pocket, or you can get the U.S. Attorney for the Middle District of Tennessee to defend them in their civil lawsuits," the preacher cautioned.

"Tom, if you'll be reasonable, we can probably make this thing disappear. What's wrong with you?" Whitehorse asked.

"If you want to me to be reasonable, don't send two braying jackasses to Ferguson to bully me or any of its citizens," Preacher Mann replied.

"Look, I'll order them back to Nashville and I'll drive up with Agent John Jenkins and we'll straighten this out. I've got another young man to talk to you about, too," Gary Simpkins offered.

"Here's the deal: I'll introduce you to Jeremy Ford. We'll entertain your questions and possibly answer those that do not tend to incriminate him. He will provide truthful answers to the questions I permit him to answer," the preacher suggested.

"Now that's reasonable," Agent Simpkins remarked.

"One more thing," the preacher said.

"What's that?" Gary Simpkins inquired.

"I'll be extending a lawful social courtesy to you and Agent Jenkins by paying for your dinner at Miss Rosie's tonight. I'll reserve you two luxury rooms and you can enjoy the Ferguson hospitality for the evening," Preacher Mann offered.

"Expect us by late afternoon. Let me talk to one of the agents," Whitehorse said.

The first agent took the phone, he listened intently for several minutes, and said, "Yes, sir. I understand."

"Now we're in big trouble, all because of you," the agent remarked.

"Beware of the ides of March," Preacher Mann warned, as the two agents exited Discount Grocery.

"A soft answer turneth away wrath," Jack Wright said with a chuckle.

The preacher replied as he made his way to the door to greet the Ford family, "A fool uttereth all his mind, but a wise man keepeth it in till afterwards."

*      *      *

Preacher Mann met with the Ford family and explained the situation to them. He alerted them about the pending investigation of Jeremy's illegal contacts on the amateur radio frequencies.

The Ford family thought it was an honor for Jeremy to serve his country despite his mobility impairment. They were relieved when Captain Anderson explained that unless east Tennessee was invaded by the enemy, Jeremy would never see combat. He opined Jeremy would very likely remain in the Knoxville area for the duration of the war.

"Have you got the enlistment paperwork with you?" Preacher Mann asked.

"We have everything necessary. After it's completed, we'll need to take him to Knoxville within a few days, get him sworn, and get his uniform and supplies from the quartermaster," Captain Anderson explained.

"I can go tonight," Jeremy said excitedly.

"You can go tomorrow. I need Captain Anderson and Sergeant Major Richmond to be in Ferguson tonight to meet my good friends, F.B.I. agents Simpkins and Jenkins.

"I will notify the executive officer at the base of our success, and explain we will be in Ferguson overnight," Captain Anderson said.

"Go down to Miss Rosie's Bed & Breakfast to reserve two rooms. Give her a U.S. Army requisition/voucher and tell her I'll help her submit the paperwork to the government for payment," Preacher Mann instructed.

"We'll just pay her, get an invoice, and request reimbursement," Captain Anderson said.

"Jeremy, make sure you pack your toothbrush. Be at Miss Rosie's by about 7:00 am. These guys get up at 5:00 am, eat breakfast about 6:00 am, and will be looking at their watches and looking for you by 7:00 am latest," Preacher Mann said.

"I'll be there. But preacher, you need to talk to Finis Lawrence about taking over all the manufacturing of the portable water heaters," Jeremy Ford replied.

"I'll tell him you're on assignment with the U.S. Army with your communications job. Everything else needs to remain with you and your parents. It's vitally important. Your work is vital to the war effort."

"Nothing will leave our lips. You can count on that," Bruce Ford, Jeremy's father stated.

\*       \*       \*

After the Fords left Community Church, Sergeant Major Richmond left in his army staff car headed for Miss Rosie's Bed & Breakfast. It wasn't very long before the preacher got there.

Shortly after 4:00 pm, Agents Gary Simpkins and John Jenkins walked into the large parlor at Miss Rosie's. Preacher Mann was reading the Friday edition of The Mountain Gazette. He looked up and saw them standing nearby.

"Two braying jackasses," Agent Jenkins said as both he and Agent Simpkins burst into hysterical laughter.

"Look, the first time I met Agent Jenkins and Agent Rogers they were very polite in seeking assistance and came with a direct introduction from you. Those two agents you sent to town were rude, threatening, and condescending," Preacher Mann explained.

"About twenty years ago you would have delivered an old-fashioned ass-whooping without regard to resorting to a civil suit," Agent Simpkins said with a chuckle.

"After law school, divinity school, and husband training, I'm more reserved," Preacher Mann responded.

"How is your beautiful wife?" Agent Jenkins queried.

"She's a big as a bear and a lot meaner," Nurse Mann said as she walked into the conversation.

"Nurse Mann, I didn't realize you were with child," Gary Simpkins remarked.

"It's worse than that. It's twins." The county nurse said with a huge smile.

"Well, Raven always excelled at everything he ever did," Gary Simpkins replied.

"I understand he called two F.B.I. agents braying jackasses, threatened them with federal civil lawsuits, and told *you* to kiss his ass," Nurse Mann reported.

"He said he's going through husband training to settle himself down," Gary Simpkins said with a chuckle.

"I suffered a setback today," Preacher Mann said sheepishly as he looked at his wife.

"Tom can't decide if he's a preacher, a lawyer, or an entrepreneur," the county nurse said.

"I'm like the Apostle Paul in that regard, 'I am made all things to all men, that I might by all means save some,'" Preacher Mann responded.

"I'm going to put my feet up in the room. Dr. Marcus Whitman said we will have two new additions to our family within a week. Finis Lawrence said we can move into the house on Monday," Nurse Mann reported.

"Anything else?" the preacher inquired.

"Yes, I'll be down to have dinner with you three promptly at 7:00 pm," she replied.

The three men stood as Nurse Mann left their presence and made her way to the large staircase in Miss Rosie's parlor. Agent Jenkins couldn't contain a huge smile.

"Whitehorse, I would recommend refraining from remarks like 'bossy little thing' or 'she's getting you trained.' Otherwise, I'll tell her what you said at dinner," the preacher warned.

"I doubt the boss will be doing any braying in Ferguson today," Agent Jenkins said with a chuckle.

"Here's the young man of the hour," Preacher Mann said as Jeremy Ford approached them.

"Hello, my name is Jeremy Ford. I understand you have some questions for me," the young man responded.

"Tom Mann has informed us he is representing you. He will be present during any questioning," Agent Jenkins said.

"Jeremy, before we begin, can you ask Captain Anderson and Sergeant Major Richmond to step in here?" Preacher Mann instructed.

"Who are they? Why are they here?" Agent Simpkins asked in rapid succession.

"Like that Wicked Witch in that recent movie, The Wizard of Oz said, 'All in good time, my little pretty,'" the preacher said, attempting to sound like the witch.

"You need us, Preacher Mann?" Captain Anderson asked.

"Agent Gary Simpkins and Agent John Jenkins meet Captain John Anderson and Sergeant Major Doug Richmond," the preacher said to introduce the four men.

After initial pleasantries were exchanged, Preacher Mann said, "Jeremy Ford is now in the United States Army and is in the custody of these two gentlemen. If you need to question him, I suggest you contact his new boss, Major General Leslie Groves. Jeremy is a Signal Corps communications officer working directly for General Groves."

"I guess this case is closed," Agent Jenkins remarked.

"No doubt," Agent Simpkins replied.

"Gentlemen, I think you three have some business to discuss. We'll bid you farewell and wish you a safe trip as you leave Ferguson," Preacher Mann said.

"Thank you, sir," Jeremy said.

"I want to say one thing, if I may," Captain Anderson said.

"It is an honor to be in the presence of two Medal of Honor recipients. Even though you aren't displaying your medals, I request that Sergeants Gary 'Whitehorse' Simpkins and Thomas 'Raven' permit us to salute you for your valor and service to our country," Captain Anderson said.

Agent Simpkins and Preacher Mann stood at attention. Captain Anderson and Sergeant Major Richmond saluted the two men who returned their salutes.

"Have a safe journey, gentlemen," Agent Simpson encouraged.

"You are just full of surprises tonight, Tom," Whitehorse said, as the two returned to their seats.

"I'm waiting for you to tell me what you wanted to talk about," the preacher replied.

"Things changed since I initially spoke to you this afternoon," Agent Simpkins announced.

"Say on," Preacher Mann said.

"We need to arrest a young man named either Joshua Bartlett Sullivan or Joshua Anderson Sullivan," Agent Simpkins responded.

"For what?" the preacher asked astonished.

"Draft evasion. He did not register for the draft. He did not respond to the draft board's notification of selection letter," Agent Simpkins reported.

"Do you know him? Can you help us locate him?" Agent Jenkins questioned.

Preacher Mann was pale and visibly shaken as Nurse Mann appeared.

"Tom, you don't look well. Are you sick?" Nurse Mann queried.

"It's the ides of March," the preacher replied.

"What in the world are you talking about?" Nurse Mann asked with concern.

"They're here to arrest Josh Sullivan for draft evasion," the preacher said bluntly.

Upon hearing the news, Nurse Mann fainted and dropped to the floor. Miss Rosie immediately made a call to Dr. Marcus Whitman's home, told him what happened, and begged for him to come quickly.

The three men placed Nurse Mann on the couch and elevated her feet. Preacher Mann held her hand and knelt beside her waiting for Dr. Whitman's arrival.

# 10. Conscription

After receiving Miss Rosie's call, Dr. Whitman arrived quickly at the bed & breakfast to attend Nurse Mann. She ushered him to the large parlor sofa where Preacher Mann and the two F.B.I. agents had placed her.

"I need everyone to exit the parlor to the dining room. Nurse Mann is entitled to privacy while I examine her and determine her condition," the physician instructed.

In about ten minutes Dr. Marcus Whitman made his way into the parlor and approached Preacher Mann. It was obvious he wasn't very happy about something.

"What's wrong with her?" Preacher Mann inquired.

"She's had a vasovagal response," the physician replied.

"What does that mean?" the preacher asked with a serious look on his face.

"She had a sudden drop in heart rate and blood pressure that led to her fainting. It happened in response to a stressful trigger," the doctor explained.

"What was the stressful trigger?" Agent Gary Simpkins inquired.

"Because her husband played a practical joke on her by telling her you two were here to arrest her preacher for draft evasion," Dr. Whitman said in an angry tone.

"Josh Sullivan is her preacher? I thought Tom was her preacher," Agent Simpkins remarked in disbelief.

"Preacher Mann is her spouse and the senior minister at Community Church. Josh Sullivan is the minister of education and the principal at the Tennessee Christian Academy," the physician explained.

"We had no idea about that," Agent John Jenkins said with astonishment.

"All three of you deserve one of those Tennessee ass-whippings the locals are always talking about. You just don't play practical jokes on a woman that's delivering twins in less than a week," Dr. Whitman opined.

"They *are* here to arrest Josh for draft evasion," Preacher Mann said.

"Tom, that's not funny. It's cruel. The last thing that young man needs is for something like that to get in The Mountain Gazette," the physician scolded.

"Actually, it's true. We have been asked to arrest the young man for draft evasion and further

investigate the case for prosecution in federal court,"
Agent Gary Simpkins remarked.

"That's the most ridiculous thing I've ever heard. A
minister of the gospel is exempt from the draft as IV-
D. I have a cousin who is a Baptist preacher. He was
just classified as exempt," Dr. Marcus Whitman
responded.

"We'll get the file from our car and go over it with
Preacher Mann. It appears there may be more to this
story than we've been told," Agent Simpkins
promised.

"No doubt," the physician said curtly.

"How's Beth? What do we need to do?" Preacher
Mann asked.

"She's fine. Miss Rosie is taking a tray of food up to
the room. I'll tell her I've updated you on her
condition, and you are working with the two agents
to straighten out the mix-up involving Josh Sullivan,"
the doctor said.

"Thanks, Dr. Whitman," Preacher Mann said as the
physician made his way to the large staircase.

"I'll get the Sullivan file from the car," Agent
Jenkins said.

"Let's find a quiet place in the parlor for our
discussion. This needs to be handled delicately due to
Brother Sullivan's visibility in the community,"
Preacher Mann stated.

"Understood," Agent Gary Simpkins replied.

When Agent Jenkins returned from the
government car with the file, Agent Simpkins said,
"Give the preacher a summary of the information in
the file. I'll ask questions when you're finished. You
can take notes for the file."

"According to the information we have, Josh
Anderson Sullivan registered for the draft while a
ministerial student at Vanderbilt Divinity School. He
dropped out of school a year ago. The local draft
board was notified, and he was reclassified.

When Joshua Sullivan's records were examined by
the draft board, they only had information on a
Joshua Bartlett Sullivan who never registered for the
draft. It appears Joshua Bartlett Sullivan is seven
months older than Joshua Anderson Sullivan claimed
on the original exemption," Agent John Jenkins
reported.

"What do the birth records from the state of
Tennessee say?" Preacher Mann inquired.

"It seems Joshua Anderson Sullivan and Joshua
Bartlett Sullivan were delivered by a doctor, Hobart
Mason, to the same mother but different fathers,"
Agent Jenkins responded.

"What happened to Joshua Bartlett Sullivan?" the
preacher asked.

"We haven't a clue. If your Joshua Sullivan has the
middle name Bartlett, he has not registered for the
draft. However, if he is, in fact, Joshua Anderson

Sullivan, his ministerial exemption was revoked when he left Vanderbilt Divinity School and then failed to respond to a draft letter from the board," Agent Jenkins said.

"How do you see the case, Tom?" Agent Simpkins inquired.

"We need to talk to Josh's parents and find out about the name discrepancy. We need to talk to Josh about his non-response to the draft board. Finally, we need to plead mistake, inadvertence, or excusable neglect to a non-response and get him exempted as a full-time minister," Preacher Mann opined.

"If he dropped out of Vanderbilt Divinity School without becoming a minister, how are you going to deal with that?" Agent Jenkins asked.

"He took his last two semesters enrolled in education courses in Middle Tennessee State Teacher's College. He will graduate with his degree in two months. He has been a full-time minister for two years at Community Church and the full-time principal at Tennessee's first correspondence high school approved by the Tennessee Board of Education," Preacher Mann explained.

"What are your thoughts on all of this, Gary?" Agent Jenkins queried.

"It's a mess. We need to talk to the local postmaster to see if Tom's Josh Sullivan actually received a letter from the draft board. We need to talk to the Sullivans to obtain the true identity of Brother Sullivan. Ultimately, this will need to be decided before a federal judge," Agent Gary Simpkins opined.

"Well, your job is to investigate, and my job is to defend. But this is one time both sides will be working toward the same ends," the preacher responded.

"We have no interest in having the U.S. Attorney for the Middle District of Tennessee prosecute a full-time minister and high school principal for draft evasion. But, that's not our call," Agent John Jenkins said.

"Let's grab some dinner and then get some rest. We can start early tomorrow by picking up Josh at The Mountain Gazette and taking him to Crab Orchard with us. Tomorrow is the day he and Louis Barrett print lesson booklets for the students," Preacher Mann instructed.

*     *     *

By 8:30 am, Josh Sullivan, Preacher Mann, Agent Gary Simpkins, and Agent John Jenkins were well on their way to the city of Crab Orchard in Cumberland County, Tennessee. It was only 28 miles from Ferguson to the Sullivan's Crab Orchard residence, but given the wartime maximum speed limit, coupled with the curvy, mountain road, the trip would be about an hour's journey.

"Josh, do you know anything about another young man named Josh Sullivan in Cumberland County? These men's records show the name as Joshua Bartlett Sullivan," Preacher Mann inquired.

"The only Sullivans I know are *my* bunch of Sullivans. We're all related. I never heard of another Josh or a Sullivan named Bart or Bartlett," the young preacher replied.

"Did you get a letter from the draft board?" Preacher Mann inquired.

"I filled out some paperwork at the Vanderbilt Divinity School. I never got a letter from anyone about those papers," Josh said.

"Think hard, Josh. If you ignored the letter, or simply forgot about it, we can deal with it. We just need to know the situation," Agent Simpkins asked.

"I never got a draft board letter. You can ask Mr. Jack Wright. He was the Acting Postmaster in Ferguson during that time. I didn't have a box, so he would hold any mail I got at the counter at Discount Grocery," Josh Sullivan responded.

"That's a good idea. That's a very good idea," Agent John Jenkins opined.

When the government car pulled into the Sullivan driveway, the four men were greeted by Opal and Bill Sullivan. They were ushered into the living room and offered fresh lemonade and cookies.

After introductions and pleasantries were exchanged, everyone was seated. Opal Sullivan seemed extremely distraught about the situation.

"There's been a mix-up at the draft board and we're here to try to straighten it out. The F.B.I. Agent-in-Charge, Gary Patrick Simpkins, and I have been friends for almost twenty-five years. We served together in The Great War, and afterward we attended law school together," Preacher Mann explained. He is here to help us sort out this situation. I ask you answer his questions honestly and fully," Preacher Mann urged.

"We understand," Bill Sullivan replied.

"Do you know a young man some seven months older than Josh Sullivan, who goes by the name of Joshua Bartlett Sullivan? Our records indicate Miss Opal is the mother of both of them," Agent Simpkins queried.

After a long pause, Bill Sullivan said, "Opal, tell the man the truth about all of this."

"In March 1917, I was engaged to a man named Joshua Bartlett. He was sent to France in April 1917 to fight in The Great War. In July of that same year, I discovered I was pregnant and on December 21, 1917, I delivered a son. Before I could notify Josh Bartlett about the pregnancy he was killed in action on June 30, 1917," Opal Sullivan explained.

"Tell him the rest of it, honey," Bill Sullivan urged.

"Bill and I had dated before I became engaged to Joshua Bartlett. Not wanting the little boy to be born out of wedlock, Bill offered to marry me, and I accepted. We were married on Thanksgiving Day 1917," Opal Sullivan continued.

"So, you named your son Joshua Bartlett Sullivan after he was delivered by Dr. Hobart Odell Mason at your home?" Agent Jenkins queried.

"Who is Joshua Anderson Sullivan?" Agent Simpkins inquired.

"That's where it gets complicated," Bill Sullivan remarked.

"We talked with Dr. Odell Mason and convinced him to create another birth certificate for Joshua Sullivan that had his birth date set as July 27, 1918," Josh's mother explained.

"Why did you do that?" Preacher Mann asked.

"Because I wanted to be Josh's father and I didn't want to always compete with a ghost. It was my ego, plain and simple," Bill Sullivan admitted.

"Where's Dr. Hobart Odell Mason now?" Agent Jenkins asked.

"He's in the Crossville City Cemetery," Opal Sullivan responded.

"He's beyond your jurisdiction, Agent Simpkins," Preacher Mann said with a chuckle.

"No doubt," Agent Jenkins added.

"My notes will reflect Joshua Bartlett is deceased and the true identity of this young man is Joshua Anderson Sullivan," Agent Simpkins noted.

"This placed him beyond his jurisdiction, too, preacher," Agent Jenkins remarked with a smile.

"Where does that leave us?" Preacher Mann asked.

"We need to talk to the acting postmaster at the time about a draft board letter. If he verifies that no letter was received in Ferguson, then Josh wouldn't be on notice to report for induction," Agent Simpkins said.

"We'd be left with getting a federal judge to overturn the draft and remand the case to the draft board for a decision on the exemption status," Agent Jenkins said.

"Can't the U.S. Attorney for the Middle District of Tennessee defer prosecution?" Preacher Mann inquired.

"He won't. It's sent down by the U.S. Army. They take draft evasion seriously. In about a year, there have been almost 3,000 draft dodgers prosecuted," Agent Simpkins opined.

"Who's the judge in this case?" Preacher Mann asked.

"You got lucky, Tom. It's Judge William Acker," Agent Gary Simpkins answered.

"Why is that good?" Josh Sullivan queried.

"Judge Acker is known for disliking the government and its lawyers. He thinks the federal government has too much power and the purpose of our Constitution, especially the Bill of Rights, serves to limit the power of the federal government," the preacher explained.

"It's in the Lord's hands and you are his faithful servant, Brother Mann," Bill Sullivan said with a break in his voice.

"Your son is his faithful servant, too," Preacher Mann responded.

"The righteous cry, and the Lord heareth, and delivereth them out of all their troubles," Gary Simpkins remarked.

"Who said that?" Bill Sullivan asked.

"Sergeant Thomas Preacher Mann on 29 September 1918, just before charging and destroying three German machine-gun emplacements near Bellicourt, France," Agent Gary Simpkins replied.

"Say on!" Josh Sullivan exclaimed.

"If I remember correctly, a U.S. Army Major watched as First Sergeant Thomas 'Raven' Mann charged the third machine-gun emplacement and was joined by Master Sergeant Gary 'Whitehorse' Simpkins. Both Raven and Whitehorse were seriously injured. The U.S. Army Major was instrumental in the two being awarded the Congressional Medal of

Honor. His name is Major William Marsh Acker, Jr.,"
Agent John Jenkins said.

*     *     *

Just as Josh had claimed, Jack Wright, acting
postmaster at the time, confirmed that no letter for
either Joshua Bartlett Sullivan or Joshua Anderson
Sullivan had been received at the U.S. Post Office in
Ferguson.

On Thursday, March 20, 1941, Lawyer Thomas P.
Mann appeared at the federal courthouse in
Cookeville for Josh Sullivan's arrest and arraignment
for violation of the Selective Service Act. He brought
the Sullivans and Jack Wright for the arraignment and
hoped to get Judge Acker to order a
contemporaneous preliminary hearing.

Agents Gary Simpkins and John Jenkins were
present with Assistant U.S. Attorney Samuel
Clements. Prosecutor Clements did not think the case
had any merit. He agreed to permit Lawyer Mann to
have as much liberty in opposing the case as Judge
Acker would allow.

The attending U.S. Marshall announced: "All rise.
United States District Court for the Middle District of
Tennessee is now in session. Judge William Acker is
presiding. God save the United States and this
honorable court. Be seated."

"The only case set for this afternoon is an arraignment in the United States versus Joshua Anderson Sullivan. Is counsel ready to proceed?" Judge Acker queried.

Both Lawyer Mann and Prosecutor Clements replied in unison, "Yes, your honor."

"I thought you were preaching, Tom," Judge Acker said with a smile.

"The government has decided to bring an absolutely bogus draft evasion case against my minister of education and principal of our Christian High School, Brother Sullivan. I move that this court accept a plea of not guilty and direct the government to provide its evidence to establish probable cause in a preliminary hearing," Preacher Mann said.

"Plea of not guilty accepted. The government is directed to present its relevant evidence in this hearing," Judge Acker ordered.

"Your honor, the government has agreed to permit me to call Agent Gary Simpkins to the stand as a hostile witness to initiate this hearing," Lawyer Mann said.

"Does the government object to this procedure?" Judge Acker queried.

"We have no objection, your honor," Prosecutor Clements replied.

"If you're going to do that, why don't you just dismiss this case and save us the trouble?" Judge Acker urged.

"I am not at liberty to dismiss this case," the prosecutor replied.

"Let's do it this way: Agent Simpkins does the government have sufficient evidence to prove probable cause in this draft evasion case?"

"After fully investigating this case, speaking with the witness, the defendant, and reviewing the alleged documents, I can assure you that the government's case is wholly without merit," Agent Simpkins said with conviction.

"Lawyer Mann, Preacher Mann, whoever in the hell you are today, what are you asking the court to do?" Judge Acker asked.

"Your honor, we request the court vacate the notice of induction and remand the case to the local draft board for a decision on an IV-D deferment," Lawyer Mann responded.

"Why don't I just find he's a minister and grant an exemption to end this circus?" Judge Acker inquired.

"I must defer to the Assistant U.S. Attorney for an answer to your question, your honor," the lawyer replied.

Judge Acker focused his eyes on the prosecutor and waited for an answer. He looked like he was ready to pounce on the Assistant U.S. Attorney.

The prosecutor said candidly, "The U.S. Army is tenacious in cases involving draft evasion. Any final ruling on exemption status will be appealed directly to the U.S. Court of Appeals for the Sixth Circuit. Lawyer Mann is acting in the interests of judicial economy."

"It's obvious the government cares nothing for judicial economy or they wouldn't have brought this case against this young preacher to start with! I'm glad Tom Mann cares about judicial economy, or I'd spend the next hour lecturing you on the proper role of government in this republic!" Judge Acker explained and then nodded at Lawyer Mann.

"Thank you, your honor," Lawyer Mann said.

Judge Acker rose and turned to leave the bench. Those present in the courtroom stood also. The federal judge removed his judicial robe and placed it on the bench in front of him.

The federal judge looked at the audience and began, "I want to say one thing to everyone present and I want this preserved on the official court record.

When two combat-wounded Congressional Medal of Honor recipients have to assist a dedicated young preacher on a trumped-up draft evasion charge like this, it's a sorry day for democracy. That's from retired Major William M. Acker, Jr. and United States District Court Judge William M. Acker, Jr."

"Say on," Preacher Mann said under his breath.

Once Judge Acker had left the courtroom, the Assistant U.S. Attorney approached Preacher Mann. He looked around the room before he began speaking.

"I doubt you've heard the end of this. The U.S. Army is quite recalcitrant. I predict they'll do their homework and provide the local draft board with reasons to deny the exemption. Most of the board members have family members serving in the military. Be prepared for a dog fight," Mr. Clements warned.

"Keep in mind what little David said before appearing with his sling and stones to battle the giant Goliath," Preacher Mann remarked.

"What was that?" Assistant U.S. Attorney Clements asked.

"Thou comest to me with a sword, and with a spear, and with a shield: but I come to thee in the name of the Lord," Agent Simpkins said.

The prosecutor nodded and walked away. Preacher Mann just gave a long stare at Agent Simpkins.

Agent Simpkins put his hand on Preacher Mann's shoulder and said, "I actually listened to those impromptu foxhole and trench sermons you preached in the war."

"Before this war is over, we both may be fighting the Germans for a second time," Agent Simpkins remarked as they walked toward the courtroom door to congratulate and encourage Brother Josh.

# 11. No Stranger There

The citizens of Ferguson experienced some highs and lows throughout 1941 and into 1942. Their experiences with the Great Depression had hardened them to withstand the deprivations and shortages inherent in World War II.

Many young men in the area had volunteered for military service. Others had been drafted to serve in the war.

Not waiting for the draft, eighteen-year-old Jackie Tubbs enlisted shortly after the attack on Pearl Harbor. He was assigned to serve in the U.S. Army Air Corps.

In April 1942, young Tubbs participated in what would come to be known as the Tokyo Raid, led by Lieutenant Colonel James H. Doolittle. It was the first strike on the Japanese homeland, and it demonstrated its vulnerability.

The Doolittle Raid boosted American morale and served as retaliation for the attack on Pearl Harbor. The mission was completed with 16 carrier-based B-25s and 80 airmen, including 52 officers and 28 enlisted men.

Even though the raid caused the loss of 15 of the B-25 bombers, most crews reached China safely. Only three men were killed in action, and eight became prisoners of war. Unfortunately, one of the heroes killed in the Tokyo Raid was bombardier Jackie Tubbs. The young man drowned when his plane crashed into the sea.

*     *     *

"Who was on the telephone?" Preacher Mann asked.

"It was Jack Wright. He needs to see you at Discount Grocery," his wife replied.

"Why? What does he want?" the preacher queried.

"He just said it was important," Nurse Mann announced.

"Get some more of that powdered baby cereal. We're almost out," the new mother requested.

"Who eats the most?" the new father asked.

"Tommy eats the most, but Johnny is not far behind. They both have your appetite," Nurse Mann remarked.

"Anything else?" the preacher inquired.

"Take that ration book and get some butter and bacon, if he has any left. You should have gotten there earlier," Nurse Mann lamented.

"Yes, dear," Preacher Mann said.

"Why do you always answer a criticism with 'Yes, dear?'" the preacher's wife asked.

158

Heading for the door, Preacher Mann responded, "It guarantees me the last word."

"Indeed," Nurse Mann said underneath her breath.

When the preacher arrived at Discount Grocery, he saw a face he hadn't seen for over a year. It was the elderly courier from the Cookeville Western Union office.

"Preacher, I know you see me as a harbinger of doom, but it's my job to get families notified about their loved ones' status," the grey-haired gentleman said apologetically.

"It's not the messenger that's upsetting. It's the messages that are contained in those telegrams," Preacher Mann said in a consoling voice.

"Who is the telegram for?" the storekeeper asked.

"It's for Jack Tubbs on Buck Mountain Road," the elderly gentleman responded.

"Do you know what it says?" Preacher Mann asked.

"They give these to me in sealed envelopes. But I can give it to the family preacher. You're at liberty to open it," the courier said.

The courier handed the telegram envelope to Preacher Mann. He nodded and turned toward the front door of Discount Grocery.

"Aren't you interested in knowing what's in the telegram?" Jack Wright asked.

"It's hard enough to deliver them. I'd just as soon stay in the dark about what they say," the old man replied.

Preacher Mann opened the telegram and read it quickly. He immediately displayed a sad countenance and said nothing.

After Preacher Mann regained his composure, he instructed, "Call Louis Barrett and tell him we're making a visit to Buck Mountain to see the Tubbs family."

*       *       *

When the preacher and the newspaper editor returned to Discount Grocery, Jack Wright inquired, "How did Jack and Martha take the loss of their son, Jackie?"

"Martha sobbed and Jack struggled to maintain his composure. It was a very, very sad situation," Louis Barrett reported.

"The longer this war lasts, the worse it will get," Preacher Mann said.

"You're going to have to start rotating deacons to make these visits. It's all I can do to not burst into tears when I see the devastation these families suffer," Louis Barrett said as he exited the building.

"What are you thinking, preacher?" Jack Wright queried.

The preacher replied, "I'm thinking about that song called, 'Gone Home.' It says:

**"All of my friends that I loved yesterday**
**Gone home (they have gone home)**
**Gone home (they have gone home)**
**The songbirds that sing in the dell seem to say**
**Gone home (they have gone home)**
**Gone home (they have gone home)**
**They've joined the heavenly fold**
**They're walking the streets of pure gold**
**They've left one by one as their work here is done**
**Gone home (they have gone home)**
**Gone home (they have gone home)"**

After a long pause, Jack Wright remarked, "'The Lord hath anointed me to preach good tidings unto the meek [and] he hath sent me to bind up the brokenhearted.' That reminds me of you, preacher."

Preacher Mann nodded and started toward the door. He had forgotten what his wife had asked him to pick up at Discount Grocery.

"Preacher don't leave yet. Your wife called and gave me some items for you to bring home. She said you'd get distracted and forget." Jack Wright reminded.

The preacher thought to himself, "The woman is dealing with a set of one-year-old twins, serving as the county nurse, and putting up with me."

Josh Sullivan walked into Discount Grocery while Jack Wright filled Preacher Mann's grocery order. Jack looked directly at the young preacher, frowned, and shook his head for him to not tell Preacher Mann about receiving a letter from the draft board.

"Here's your order. I'll see you tomorrow for services at the church," Jack Wright said cheerfully.

Noting Josh Sullivan's presence, Preacher Mann responded, "Come to early service. Josh is delivering the message," Preacher Mann instructed.

"I am! What's the reason for that?" Josh asked with a degree of surprise.

"Because you didn't have to tell Jack and Martha Tubbs on a Saturday their son died in Doolittle's Raid on Tokyo," the preacher replied as he left the store with his bag of groceries.

"That's awful," Josh Sullivan exclaimed.

Hold that draft board letter till late next week. You don't have to appear for thirty days. The preacher's grief wagon is overflowing today," Jack Wright instructed.

"No doubt," the young preacher replied.

Unknown to Josh Sullivan, Jack Wright had received an audit letter from the Office of Price Administration that oversaw the local rationing board. He intended to wait until Monday afternoon to ask the preacher for his help.

*   *   *

Josh Sullivan preached the 9:00 am service and taught the Bible study class. Preacher Mann finished the morning by bringing the message at 11:00 am. He concluded the service by announcing the heroic death of Jackie Tubbs, and he had a congregational prayer for his family.

Miss Rosie offered to watch the twins at the Mann's home on Sunday evening. Preacher Mann and his wife decided to take a short trip to Smithville, Tennessee and stay at a cabin on the Caney Fork River overnight.

The trip was mostly about an opportunity for the couple to obtain some rest from their hectic life and the attention required by the twins. They were unaware of anything that happened in Ferguson until Sheriff John C. 'Chub' Hill showed up at their door.

"I'm sorry to disturb you and your wife, preacher. But something serious has happened in Ferguson overnight. I got an early call from Sheriff Hankins," Sheriff Hill said apologetically.

"What's the problem in Ferguson?" Preacher Mann inquired.

"It seems that someone broke into Discount Grocery late Sunday night or early Monday morning and, under cover of darkness, they emptied the storeroom and a lot of merchandise from the shelves," Sheriff Hill explained.

"That's horrible," Nurse Mann exclaimed.

"It gets worse. When he got there this morning, the store owner became so distraught that he suffered a massive heart attack. He may not make it. Sheriff Hankins thinks you should come as quickly as possible," the sheriff reported.

"Where's Jack Wright being cared for?" Nurse Mann asked.

"Sheriff Hankins said for you to come to Dr. Whitman's clinic. He's there," Sheriff Hill responded.

"We appreciate your delivering the message. We'll be on our way shortly," Preacher Mann assured Sheriff Hill.

The trip from Smithville to Ferguson was only about 42 miles. But with a 35 mile per hour speed limit and a wartime gasoline scarcity, the journey would take close to an hour-and-a-half.

When the couple arrived at the clinic located in Smith's Apothecary, they were immediately met by Joe Scott. He shook his head indicating Jack Wright's condition was serious.

"I'll get Marcus. He wanted to talk to you before you saw Jack," the pharmacist said.

"That was not a good sign. I hope Dr. Whitman is more optimistic," the county nurse remarked.

When Dr. Marcus Whitman, followed by Joe Scott, approached the Manns, his demeanor was sad. It was not his usual, somewhat pleasant, countenance.

He looked at Preacher Mann and reported, "He's alive but in serious condition. I'll think he'll live through this, but Jack is convinced he's going to die."

"What happened?" Nurse Mann asked.

"It appears that a blood clot of unknown size has partially blocked the left anterior descending artery of his heart," the physician reported.

"The widowmaker," the county nurse gasped.

"What can you do?" the preacher asked.

"I can give him some blood-thinning drugs that may dislodge or dissolve the clot. Given his situation, I think there's a good chance he'll survive. However, if I've misjudged the size of the clot, or its location, he'll likely die," the doctor reported.

"So, it's not truly a widowmaker but very similar," Nurse Mann said.

"Exactly," the physician opined.

"We were told that the store burglary caused the heart attack," Preacher Mann remarked.

"I'm sure the stress of rationing, shortages of stock, record keeping requirements, service deaths of local youth, and the store burglary, contributed to his recent coronary troubles. But I can't place them as the direct cause. It's probably as much heredity, diet, and lifestyle as anything," remarked Dr. Marcus Whitman.

"What do you need me to do?" Preacher Mann asked.

"Stay with him. Talk to him. Encourage him to get some rest. Pr

ay hard for him. My intervention consists of getting that clot, or blockage dissolved," Dr. Whitman instructed.

Dr. Whitman led Preacher Mann and his wife to the clinic bedside of Jack Wright. He looked up and cast a large smile in the preacher's direction.

"I didn't think you'd get here before I left this world," Jack Wright said.

"I'm told that if you do as you're told you'll be back on your feet by the end of the week. I'm here to enforce Dr. Whitman's rules," Preacher Mann said.

"I thought you were a preacher, not a policeman," Jack Wright said with a chuckle.

"I'm following Paul's instruction to Timothy: 'Reprove, rebuke, and exhort.' Just remember, that recipe is two-thirds negative and one-third positive," the preacher responded.

"Nurse Mann and I are going to leave you two alone. I don't want to see or hear what's going to happen if you run afoul of the preacher," Dr. Whitman remarked.

After Dr. Whitman and Nurse Mann left Jack Wright's bedside, the merchant said, "Now I know you can't lie, not even to a dying man, I want to ask you something important."

"Say on," the preacher replied.

"Am I going to die?" Jack Wright asked earnestly.

"Eventually, unless Jesus returns in your lifetime," Preacher Mann said.

"I mean from this heart attack," Jack Wright insisted.

"Dr. Whitman said your condition is serious. He thinks you will survive it. He is giving you medicine to dissolve the small clot that is blocking an artery," the preacher reported.

"I just don't think I'm going to make it," the storekeeper lamented.

"I wasn't aware you'd graduated from medical school and had treated hundreds of heart patients," Preacher Mann said somewhat sarcastically.

"Well, I haven't but. . .," the merchant continued before he was interrupted by the preacher.

"Hogwash! Get some rest before I really give you a fire and brimstone sermon to remember," Preacher Mann insisted.

Jack Wright lay in the clinic bed and stared at the ceiling. He hesitated to ask the preacher anything, but he felt he had no choice.

"I need to talk to you about something," Jack Wright said.

"No, I am not bringing you any moonshine," the preacher said sternly.

"I didn't realize that was an option," Jack Wright said with a smile.

"What do you really want to discuss?" the preacher queried.

"I got a letter from the rations board. They're sending an auditor to audit my records next week. I'm deficient," Jack Wright said.

"What do you mean that you're deficient?" Preacher Mann asked with a puzzled look.

"With the help of Henry Wooden, I've been dealing gray market and occasionally black market goods. I don't have the ration coupons to cover the overages," the storekeeper explained.

"Are you desirous of confessing your sins to Preacher Mann, or are you seeking representation from Lawyer Mann?" the preacher inquired.

"Both," Jack Wright replied.

"I'll tell Henry Wooden to send his accountant to the store to straighten out your records," Preacher Mann said.

"What about the missing ration coupons?" Jack Wright asked.

"Jehovah Jireh with a little help from Henry Wooden," Preacher Mann said with a chuckle.

"Sometimes it's hard for me to tell when you're being Preacher Mann or Lawyer Mann," Jack Wright remarked.

"It's only important that I know the difference," the preacher said.

The rest of the afternoon was uneventful for the preacher and the merchant. It was difficult for the preacher to keep from nodding off, but the shopkeeper refused to close his eyes.

"I noticed you're nodding off. Were you and the nurse working on another set of twins at the river cabin last night?" Jack Wright queried.

"You're improving," the preacher remarked.

"Why do you say that?" Jack Wright inquired.

"You are back to being the cub reporter for The Mountain Gazette," Preacher Mann said with a slight degree of irritation.

Jack Wright clutched his chest and had difficulty catching his breath. The preacher realized quickly this was a serious situation. He moved to the clinic door and yelled for Dr. Whitman.

Both Dr. Marcus Whitman and Joe Scott arrived in the clinic simultaneously. Nurse Mann was only a step or two behind them.

"He clutched his chest and started having serious difficulty breathing," Preacher Mann reported.

"Joe, you and the preacher, step out of the room. Nurse Mann, we are going to directly inject near the clot," Dr. Whitman instructed.

Preacher and Joe Scott stepped out of the clinic into the apothecary. They listened intently and heard a loud groan from Jack Wright.

"What happened?" the preacher asked as Dr. Whitman made his way out of the clinic.

"The clot has moved and is now only partially blocking the artery, or at least it's smaller than it was," Dr. Whitman said.

"That sounds encouraging," Joe Scott opined.

"I directly injected some blood-thinning medication at a site near the clot. If the clot is dissolving, the medication may make it go away quicker," Dr. Whitman said.

"What's the worst-case scenario?" Preacher Mann queried.

"The clot dislodges and creates another blockage, and this one kills him," Dr. Whitman said bluntly.

"What do you think?" Joe Scott queried.

"He's in a mostly stable condition. He's not out of the woods but I think the medication is working," the physician opined.

When the preacher returned to the clinic room, Jack Wright asked, "What did the doctor say?"

"He said the clot is dissolving. He gave you an injection of blood thinner directly in the area of the clot to dissolve it more quickly," Preacher Mann reported.

"What did he say about me dying?" the merchant inquired.

"He said you were too mean to die." Preacher Mann replied.

"I don't believe it," Jack Wright said with a slight amount of irritation.

"If you die, I'll make sure they put an epitaph on your tombstone says, 'Dr. Marcus Whitman was wrong,'" the preacher promised.

Jack Wright turned away from the preacher and grunted. The preacher had to stifle a laugh.

After several minutes of the cold shoulder, the merchant turned onto his back. He stated he had another question for the preacher.

"No, I'm not slipping that Lewis girl in for a visit, even though you might die with a smile on your face that the undertaker couldn't erase," Preacher Mann said.

"After that remark, it's obvious that you, at least, think I'm improving," Jack Wright said.

"What's your question?" the preacher asked.

"Will we know each other in heaven?" the shopkeeper queried.

"Absolutely," Preacher Mann said.

"How do you know that? How can you be sure?" Jack Wright asked in rapid succession.

"On the Mount of Transfiguration, Peter, James and John, recognized the prophets Moses and Elijah. At the empty tomb, Mary Magdalene recognized Jesus when she turned around after he spoke to her," Preacher Mann replied.

It was obvious this illness had taken a toll on the merchant. He needed to rest, but he feared if he closed his eyes he would not wake up in mortality. He stared at the ceiling while the preacher remained at his bedside.

As the afternoon turned into evening, the Smith Brothers Band showed up at the clinic door to let the merchant know he was in their prayers. They did not bring their instruments. Jack Wright was facing away from the clinic door and toward the wall.

"Turn over, Jack. The Smith Brothers are here to pay their last respects," the preacher said in a loud voice.

When Cecil, Randall, and the boys saw Jack Wright, it was obvious he was in bad shape. In fact, Doris Smith had to step away from the clinic door to prevent him from seeing the tears in her eyes.

"Jack needs to hear a song from you," Preacher Mann announced.

"We didn't bring our instruments. We weren't expecting to play a concert," Cecil Smith said with a smile.

"You can do it acapella. You know it well. It's an old hymn called, 'I'll Be No Stranger There.'"

Cecil nodded and the Smith Brothers Band began:

"I know I'll be no stranger yonder
In that Holy City fair
I know I'll be (You know I'll be)
No stranger there (No stranger there)
I'll see my Jesus and my loved ones
And my friends will all be there
(I'll be no stranger) Praise the Lord when I get there

(I'll be no stranger) Be no stranger there
(On Heaven's shore) On that golden shore
(We'll know each other) Know each other there
(As on earth before) As on earth before
(You'll see me walk) Walkin' down the street
(No place to go) To reach that shining shore
(Down by the river) Down by that river fair
(With the saints of old) With the saints of old."

During the song, Jack Wright seemed to relax for
the first time that day. When they had concluded the
song, Preacher Mann nodded his head for them to
move out of the clinic room.

Jack Wright motioned for Preacher Mann to move
closer so he could tell him something. The preacher
obliged and placed his ear closer to the merchant's
lips.

"You are the only real friend I've ever had. If the
Lord calls me home tonight, I'll be there waiting for
you," Jack Wright said as he drifted off to sleep.

When he lifted his head, the preacher's eyes had filled with tears. He would later write in his journal that, at that instant, he felt as though he had fulfilled the words of the psalmist, "there is a friend that sticketh closer than a brother."

# 12. Quid Pro Quo

Despite the ongoing war in the European and Pacific Theatres, the next year in Ferguson saw, at least locally, a period of return to near-normal life in the little mountain town.

After a week of bed rest, Dr. Marcus Whitman approved Jack Wright's return to light duty at Discount Grocery. Brother Josh Sullivan and Preacher Mann alternated days to help Frankie Wright manage the store until Jack Wright was back on his feet. The two preachers continued to help for a month afterward by unpacking freight and stocking shelves during the merchant's recovery period.

Preacher Mann appeared with Josh Sullivan at the local draft board. He convinced the board to delay a decision on Josh's ministerial deferment to a future date when his draft lottery number was actually reached.

Fortunately, Preacher Mann was not tasked with delivering any killed in action or missing in action telegrams to Ferguson families during those few months. In future years, he remarked that World War

II was the worst time he had experienced as minister of the gospel.

The Mann's twins, Tommy and Johnny, continued to grow and provide a large measure of happiness to their parents during a bleak period in their lives. By the summer of 1943, they were both walking and talking. The preacher remarked they were already preparing to be missionaries.

*    *    *

"I see you're back to Monday as your day off," Jack Wright remarked as the preacher walked into Discount Grocery.

"How could you tell?" Preacher Mann asked with a smile.

"You're not wearing preacher clothes. That means you're not making any visits or preacher rounds. Those are street clothes and not work clothes. That means you're not doing any 'Honey Do' chores for your wife," the merchant opined.

"Was there anything else?" the preacher inquired.

"Yeah, Josh stopped by this morning and picked up a ham sandwich and a can of beans for lunch. He said you had today off, but he was printing lesson booklets with Louis Barrett," Jack Wright replied.

"Your mind is like a steel trap," Preacher Mann remarked as he rolled his eyes.

"That's right. I'm sharp. But I don't always reveal my sources," Jack Wright replied.

"It's time," the preacher said.

"Time for what?" the storekeeper asked.

"It's time for Louis Barrett to promote you from cub reporter to news correspondent," Preacher Mann opined.

"I suppose that's a compliment," Jack Wright mused.

Josh Sullivan walked into Discount Grocery. He was not his usual cheerful self.

"Need more lunch?" Jack Wright asked.

"I lost my appetite when I picked up this registered letter at the post office. It says you are getting a copy, too," Josh reported.

"Is it from Nurse Abby's parents about whether you have honorable intentions toward her?" Preacher Mann asked while both he and Jack Wright chuckled.

"This is serious. The draft board has set a hearing to revoke my ministerial exemption. It's ten days from now," the young preacher reported.

"Let me make a few calls and find out what's going on. Keep printing your lesson booklets," Preacher Mann instructed.

Josh nodded and handed the letter to Preacher Mann. His mood was slightly improved as he left the store.

"Looks like your day off has been canceled," Jack Wright opined.

"If you don't mind, I want to make a couple of calls on your phone. The twins have colds and Beth is on sick leave today. There's no way I can make calls from that madhouse," the preacher reported.

"These are the good times. Wait till they start chasing girls and some concerned parents want to talk with you," Jack Wright warned.

"I was wrong about your becoming a news correspondent. You should opt for an advice column," Preacher Mann said as he walked toward the wall phone.

*     *     *

The Selective Service Act of December 20, 1941 made all men between the ages of 20 and 44 liable for military service. The Act required all men between the ages of 18 and 64 to register.

By December 5, 1942, the conscriptions were limited by executive order to 18-38. Men that were at least 18 could voluntarily enlist as well as men older than draft age.

Preacher Mann enlisted F.B.I. Agent Gary Simpkins to speak with the Assistant U.S. Attorney about the situation at the draft board. Even though Josh's hearing was only at the administrative stage, an unofficial inquiry might reveal some useful information.

Additionally, the preacher contacted Captain John Anderson at the U.S. Army Corp of Engineers facility near Knoxville, Tennessee. He hoped to see whether the pressing draft issue was related just to Josh Sullivan or whether it was a general surge in conscription due to the need for more combatants.

By the middle of the week, the preacher had received reports from his friends at the F.B.I. office in Nashville and the Army Corps of Engineers at the Clinton Engineering Works near Knoxville. The reports did not bode well for Josh Sullivan.

It seemed the young preacher was facing two major issues. First, after defeating the Germans in North Africa and Italy, the U.S. Army needed to increase the number of soldiers in preparation for the invasion of Europe. Second, Josh Sullivan's lottery number had been drawn and his ministerial exemption was questioned since the small town of Ferguson already had one preacher – Preacher Mann.

"What are you going to do about Josh's situation?" Nurse Mann asked at the dinner table on Thursday evening.

"I'm going to take Whitehorse and go see Major General Leslie Groves tomorrow. The man thinks he owes me a couple of favors. I intend to cash in those chips," Preacher Mann remarked.

"What do you intend to try to get him to do?" the preacher's wife asked.

"It's like that Wicked Witch in the Wizard of Oz movie we saw in Cookeville said, 'But that's not what's worrying me. It's how to do it. These things must be done delicately,'" Preacher Mann said attempting to mimic the movie character.

"The hourglass is running out of sand, Dorothy," Nurse Mann replied.

*    *    *

The next morning Agent Gary Simpkins and Preacher Mann left Ferguson early to be at General Groves' office at 10:30 am. A trip from Ferguson to Clinton Engineering Works was about 71 miles or slightly over two hours, not taking into account that Ferguson was in the central time zone and the Knoxville area was in the eastern time zone. Given the terrain and the 35 mph speed limit, in an abundance of caution, the pair left the Mann home at 6:00 am local time.

"Tom, you always find a way to get into these situations and I get dragged into them with you," Agent Simpkins lamented.

"You're the guy who talked me into going to law school. Therefore, this is your fault," Preacher Mann replied.

"Well, other than charging machine-gun nests in France, most of your shenanigans have occurred after you became a preacher," Agent Simpkins observed.

"Did you join the 'moan and groan club' today?" the preacher asked with slight irritation.

"If this general decides your request constitutes our participation in a conspiracy to help Josh Sullivan evade the draft, you'll be doing moaning and groaning, too," Agent Simpkins replied.

"The king's heart is in the hand of the Lord, as the rivers of waters: he turneth it whithersoever he will," Preacher Mann said, quoting from Proverbs.

"You'd better pray hard he turns those rivers on you when General Groves starts blistering your ass over this case," Agent Simpkins said emphatically as he parked the car at the Clinton Engineering Works.

Both Gary 'Whitehorse' Simpkins and Thomas 'Raven' Mann entered the reception area wearing their Congressional Medals of Honor. The staff sergeant at the desk stood and saluted the pair.

"We're here to see General Groves," Agent Simpkins said.

"He is in his office with Captain John Anderson. I've been instructed to admit both of you when you arrive," the desk sergeant replied.

The sergeant knocked on General Groves' door and heard the word, enter. He announced the arrival of the pair and motioned for them to enter.

181

Upon seeing the two Congressional Medal of Honor winners displaying their medals, and for military courtesy, both General Groves and Captain Anderson stood and saluted the men. The salutes were returned in true military fashion.

"Be seated, gentlemen. I doubt any other general has had the privilege to entertain two Congressional Medal of Honor recipients in his office at the same time. This is a privilege, Raven and Whitehorse," General Groves said.

"We appreciate your taking the time to see us. This is an important matter for both of us," Agent Gary Simpkins offered.

"Captain Anderson has briefed me about the situation with your young protégé, Preacher Mann. The problem is not the U.S. Army per se. It is the regulations pertaining to exemptions," General Groves said.

"Can you explain that, sir?" Preacher Mann queried.

"Captain give us the short version," the general instructed.

"Josh Sullivan is not a full-time pastor or minister as contemplated by regulations promulgated to enforce the Selective Service Act. He is employed in a para-ministry operation. He left his studies in divinity school and opted for a teaching degree. This disqualified him for a ministry student exemption.

He operates a state-approved correspondence high school that bears the name Tennessee Christian Academy. It is neither a congregation nor a school that trains ministers. He preaches for you occasionally but not full-time for any congregation.

You are the full-time minister at Community Church. Since you are approaching 43 years of age, you are currently exempted from the draft by executive order. In summation, Josh Sullivan is going to be drafted," Captain John Anderson reported.

Preacher Mann and Agent Simpkins nodded their heads negatively in disbelief. They obviously disagreed with the draft board's position.

"I can tell you this war is a long way from over. General Eisenhower is amassing forces for an invasion of Europe. It will cost many American lives to defeat the Nazis. The Battle of Midway moved the Japanese fleet three thousand miles back toward their mainland. But defeating them will be just as difficult. It could even be bloodier than liberating Europe," General Groves
explained.

"Captain Anderson, do we have any other options?" Agent Simpkins asked.

"Josh Sullivan has the option of applying for conscientious objector status. Given his work, he'd be a good candidate for that exemption," the captain replied.

"I don't consider that an option," Agent Simpkins remarked.

"Neither do I," Preacher Mann responded.

"Notwithstanding this report I got from Captain Anderson, I am willing to make a direct appeal to the General of the Army, George Marshall," General Groves offered.

"That would be wonderful," Preacher Mann exclaimed.

"Yes, it would," Agent Simpkins said excitedly.

"What I'm about to tell you is highly classified. Only a handful of people in this country know of its existence. I received approval from General Marshall, who received approval directly from the president, to share this information with you. If it is divulged, you will be subject to prosecution," General Groves warned.

"Say on," Preacher Mann replied.

"Indeed," Agent Gary Simpkins said in agreement.

"I have been tasked with overseeing what is called The Manhattan Project. Clinton Engineering Works is a top-secret research facility that will produce the first nuclear weapon or atomic bomb. It is a weapon so powerful and destructive that one bomb could destroy a city of up to a quarter-million people. It could end the war in the Pacific theater upon deployment," General Groves explained.

"How long will it take?" Preacher Mann asked.

"The Army Corps of Engineers is acquiring 60,000 acres of land in this area and we hope to hope to quickly begin construction thereafter. Our best time frame to develop and deploy the bomb is in late 1944 or early 1945," the general responded.

"How do you intend to keep an operation like this secret?" Agent Gary Simpkins inquired.

Our head of security is Major Bud Uanna. He's a security expert. We have absolute confidence in him.

"Respectfully, General, how does that involve us?" Agent Simpkins inquired.

"Bud Uanna is a good man. To do this job he needs good men to help him. I've got an F.B.I. agent and a preacher with a law degree in my office. I need one to work in security and one to work as a chaplain and legal officer. It's that simple. I can't get you drafted but I can pressure you to volunteer to save tens of thousands of lives," General Leslie Groves urged.

"We're old. It's been almost 25 years since we've been in the military," the preacher replied.

"I'd say you're seasoned. Hell, you both are younger than me," General Groves said with a chuckle.

"With your permission, General Groves," Captain Anderson interjected.

General Groves nodded affirmatively, and Captain Anderson continued, "If the two of you volunteer for service at this facility, you will receive field commissions as captains and be detailed directly to the Manhattan Project. Josh Sullivan will become the full-time preacher at Community Church and qualify for the ministerial exemption."

"I'll explain the situation to General George Mitchell. It'll be one of those 'one hand washes the other' deals. The draft board will receive a confidential letter explaining that Josh Sullivan is the full-time minister of two Congressional Medal of Honor recipients who have re-enlisted to serve their country. As you two lawyers say in Latin, it's quid pro quo or a little something for something," General Groves explained.

Agent Gary Simpkins looked directly at Preacher Mann and said, "I told you this morning, you always find a way to get into these situations, and I get dragged into them with you!"

"When do we have to report for duty?" Preacher Mann asked.

"Once you enlist, you'll have thirty days to report for duty. Although your enlistment paperwork will mention two years, it'll actually be for the duration of hostilities," Captain John Anderson explained.

"I've got an eighteen-month-old set of twins. What part of this can I share with my wife?" Preacher Mann asked.

"Ouch! You may qualify for combat pay without leaving the states," Captain Anderson remarked.

"You can tell her that you responded to a direct appeal from Lieutenant General Leslie Groves for the two of you to assist with duties at a secret base near Knoxville. You can say that you will not be deployed anywhere except that location. You can tell her that it caused the army to intervene with the draft board on Josh Sullivan's behalf," the general explained.

"Can I tell her anything else?" Preacher Mann asked.

"That you've only got thirty days to kiss and make up," General Groves said with a chuckle.

"Since she's a nurse, I'm confident that we can find her a position on the base," Captain John Anderson offered.

"He had better not pick that scab for a few months," Agent Simpkins opined.

"Sergeant bring in those enlistment papers for these two gentlemen. I'll personally administer the oath," General Groves bellowed.

"How did you know the fish would bite?" Preacher Mann asked.

"I know the fish," General Groves replied.

*     *     *

As they reached the halfway point from the military base to Ferguson, Agent Gary Simpkins asked, "Do you think it would help if I spent the night and helped explain this situation to your wife?"

"It's like a friend taking a friend home drunk. To his wife, the friend is the cause of her loving husband coming home inebriated. She'll turn the wrath of God loose on you, brother," Preacher Mann reasoned.

"I'm dropping you off in the driveway. I'll see you at the base in thirty days," Agent Simpkins replied.

When Preacher Mann walked in the front door he was met by his beautiful wife with a hug and a kiss. He couldn't hear any happy or unhappy toddler noise and they weren't to be seen.

"Where are the kids?" Preacher Mann inquired.

"They're spending the night at Miss Rosie's. She's playing grandma again," Nurse Mann replied.

"Why is she doing that?" the preacher queried.

"She said I needed to give you some love and celebrate if you were successful," his wife announced.

"What if I was unsuccessful?" Preacher Mann asked.

"She said in that case, I needed to give you twice as much love and console you," Nurse Mann responded.

"Indeed," the preacher said slightly beneath his breath.

"So, is it a single scoop or a double scoop of loving tonight?" the county nurse asked with a large smile.

"I doubt they'll be much loving tonight," the preacher announced sadly.

"Why do you say that?" Beth Mann asked with uncertainty in her voice.

"General Groves lobbied General Marshall, the General of the Army, to confidentially direct the draft board to exempt Josh Sullivan," Preacher Mann said.

"You may get a double scoop anyway," his wife responded.

"Josh could not qualify because he was not a full-time minister for any congregation," Preacher Mann said before he was interrupted.

"Titles are not important. You can switch positions during the war. The board of deacons can name him the minister. You're too old to be drafted," Nurse Mann opined.

"General Groves said this is what I must say to you: Gary 'Whitehorse' Simpkins and Thomas 'Raven" Mann responded to a direct appeal from Lieutenant General Leslie Groves for us to assist with duties at a secret base near Knoxville. We will not be deployed anywhere except that location. It caused the United States Army to directly intervene with the draft board on Josh Sullivan's behalf," Preacher Mann reported.

"When do you have to report for duty?" Nurse Mann asked.

"We have been given thirty days before reporting," the preacher said somberly.

"I have an idea why the two of you did this. You are both American heroes. You put the good of this

country before your personal well-being. I just
wanted to hear it from you," his wife said tearfully.

"General Eisenhower is amassing an invasion force
to take the battle to the Germans. General MacArthur
is fighting the Japanese in bloody naval and land
battles in the Pacific. The outcome of this war is far
from decided.

Your husband and his best friend are convinced
that, not only will their service as U.S. Army captains
keep Josh Sullivan out of harm's way, the nature of
their duties at Oak Ridge could help prevent the loss
of tens of thousands of lives, and help the war
conclude sooner.

There is no victory without sacrifice. It is the nature
of war.

Across this country, in tens of thousands of homes,
husbands, fathers, sons and brothers are fighting
tyranny in Europe and in the Pacific. Why should
Gary Simpkins and Thomas Mann sit in the comfort
of their homes, enjoy the fruits of democracy, and
ignore the call of their country?

This is the right thing to do. It is the honorable
thing to do. It is the only thing to do." Preacher Mann
said eloquently.

Nurse Mann stood and began to walk away from
the foyer and into the living room. She faced away
from the preacher.

"Let's go!" Nurse Mann said bluntly.

"Are we going to pick up the children?" Preacher Mann asked.

"I'm going to feed you dinner and you're getting two scoops for dessert," his wife promised.

"Let's skip dinner and go for three scoops," the preacher suggested.

"Say on," the nurse said with a giggle.

# 13. Whither Thou Goest

When the preacher opened his eyes, he immediately reached for his watch. Much to his surprise, it was half-past eight. It had been a long time since he'd slept that late – even on a Saturday morning.

He looked at the other side of the bed and his wife wasn't there. He wondered if there was a problem with the twins but then remembered they had spent the night with Miss Rosie.

"Beth! Have you run away with another man?" Preacher Mann asked in a loud voice.

"I'll be there in a minute," his wife replied.

Within a couple of minutes, Nurse Mann entered the room clad in a very sheer white teddy. It didn't leave much to the imagination.

"How do you like it?" she asked.

"Did you get a discount?" Preacher Mann asked.

"It's a Clayton Martin original. Why would I get a discount?" she asked with a very puzzled look.

"Based upon the amount of fabric, coupled with the fact it's as thin as tissue paper, I thought he might

have discounted the price," the preacher remarked
with a chuckle.

"SheMammy made it especially for your birthday.
I decided I'd wear it a few weeks early," Nurse Mann
replied with a wink.

"I guess I'll take a shower, get dressed, and greet
the day," Preacher Mann remarked.

"I've already groomed, put on this sexy lingerie,
and cooked your breakfast," Nurse Mann replied.

"I must have been sound asleep. I didn't hear any
of that," the preacher said.

"You were in a love coma," his wife said as she
turned to leave the bedroom.

"I guess it was that third scoop of ice cream," the
preacher remarked.

While he was in the shower, the preacher became
convinced he could smell country ham frying. But he
blamed it on his imagination. He hadn't had country
ham, sausage, or bacon for breakfast since Jack
Wright's heart attack.

His wife had scolded him for getting a spare tire
around his waist and clogging his veins with fatty
foods. It was oatmeal, cereal, and an occasional
poached egg and toast for breakfast.

After the preacher had dressed and made his way
to the kitchen, he discovered, much to his delight, his
plate had a huge slab of country ham, two scrambled

eggs, a serving of grits, and three biscuits. He was thankful but suspicious.

"What happened to my heart-healthy diet?" Preacher Mann asked as he seated himself at the table.

"It's suspended presently. You've taken off almost twenty pounds and you have been diligent in changing your eating habits," his wife replied.

"This is almost a spiritual experience," the preacher said as he began to devour his meal.

"Aren't you going to say a blessing?" his wife queried.

"I give thanks every time I take a bite," the preacher said with a smile.

The preacher didn't speak during the meal. He always said he could eat or talk but not do either very well at the same time. Jack Wright said the preacher never wasted time while eating. He only tasted the first few bites before shoveling in the balance of the meal.

After finishing his big breakfast, the preacher said jokingly, "What else have you got?"

"I have a special treat for you," his wife responded.

"I like the sound of that," the preacher said with a wink.

"Look at the back of the card at the center of the table," she instructed.

195

The preacher picked up the notecard and read its contents. It contained a portion of a Bible verse that read: "For whither thou goest, I will go; and where thou lodgest, I will lodge."

There was a long, silent pause before the preacher spoke. He knew the meaning of the verse his wife had written on the card. She intended to take the twins and move to Oak Ridge with him.

"Aren't you going to say anything?" Nurse Mann asked.

"No ma'am!" Preacher Mann replied.

Nurse Mann arose from her seat, approached her husband, and gave him a long hug and a kiss. Years later Nurse Mann would blame the preacher's lack of resistance on the teddy designed by SheMammy, coupled with the big country ham breakfast. Preacher Mann always said he knew it was futile to try to change her mind.

"What are your plans for the day?" Nurse Mann asked.

"I've got to update Josh on the situation. I've got to advise the deacons today and the congregation tomorrow about the enlistment. I've got to talk with George Hickman about this house," the preacher reported.

"Josh has got news for you, too. He's graduating from Middle Tennessee State Teachers College next month. He and Abby are getting married and he expects you to do the honors," Nurse Mann announced.

"I had a good, long talk with him several months ago. Is it one of those 'oops' situations?" Preacher Mann queried.

"She's not pregnant, if that's what you mean," Nurse Mann replied.

"When's the special day?" the preacher asked with a chuckle.

"I'd say within the next thirty days," Nurse Mann offered.

"He'll be finding out his pay will increase when he becomes the senior minister," the county nurse remarked.

"Indeed," the preacher said.

"George Hickman will certainly let him make the payments on this house while we're in the military," Nurse Mann opined.

"You mean while I'm in the military, don't you?" Preacher Mann said attempting to correct his wife.

"Last night you commented that Captain John Anderson offered a position for me, but you told him you wouldn't 'pick that scab' because you thought I would be upset about your re-enlistment," the nurse replied.

"That is correct. But what is your point?" the preacher asked.

"While you were in your love coma, I called the base at 7:00 am and asked for Captain Anderson. I discussed our situation with him, and he made an appointment for me to meet with Captain Charles T. Lowe, the chief medical officer at the base on Monday afternoon," Nurse Mann reported.

"Well, being a civilian employee isn't a bad job. It will help you keep up your nursing skills for the next two years or so," Preacher Mann opined.

"I'm planning on being commissioned as a nurse in the U.S. Army. If I'm a staff nurse, I'll be a first lieutenant. If Dr. Lowe chooses for me to serve as the charge or head nurse, I'll make captain," Nurse Mann reported.

"Now Beth, if you take a commission, the army will own your soul for the enlistment period. It can call on you at any time day or night, weekends, holidays, for double shifts, etc.," the preacher said in an attempt to explain what she was considering.

"I've already thought about that. It's why we're going to the Bluebird Café to see Ruth Bell this morning," the preacher's wife announced.

"What's any of this got to do with Miss Ruth?" Preacher Mann queried.

"Unknown to you, she's been helping with the twins and doing some maid work one-half day a week. She mentioned she wished she had a full-time job taking care of this house and the twins every day," the nurse remarked.

"You want Ruth Bell to be our live-in maid and nanny?" Preacher Mann asked with a degree of incredulity.

"Like General Leslie Groves, I have confidence in your ability to get things done," Nurse Mann said.

"No doubt," the preacher replied as he took his breakfast plate to the sink.

\*     \*     \*

When the preacher and his wife arrived at the Bluebird Café, the restaurant was packed with the breakfast crowd. The parking lot was completely full, and they had to park Preacher Mann's truck beneath the oak tree outside the kitchen entrance.

Preacher Mann knocked on the door and was met by Cecil Smith. He was surprised to see the preacher for breakfast since he'd been on the no-country-ham diet.

"Have you slipped away from Nurse Mann and come into the kitchen for a couple of country ham biscuits to eat on the sly?" Cecil Smith asked with a hearty laugh.

Overhearing the conversation, Nurse Mann stepped into the doorway and said, "He's off dietary restrictions as of today. I fed him a full slab of ham and biscuits for breakfast."

"He's definitely looking fit and trim," Cecil Smith remarked.

"I need to talk seriously about something," Preacher Mann said, motioning Cecil to sit on the slatted wooden bench beneath the huge oak tree.

When he had taken a seat, Cecil Smith said, "Say on."

"What I'm about to tell you is strictly confidential. I have not told Josh or the deacon's board. Beth is the only person who is aware of the situation," Preacher Mann explained.

"You can count on me. I won't say a word if Clarence Hankins tied me up and beat me," Cecil Smith promised.

"At the specific request of the base commander in Knoxville, Agent Gary Simpkins and I have re-enlisted in the U.S. Army. Beth is planning on serving as a nurse on the base. We'll be leaving Ferguson for two years in about thirty days," Preacher Mann said.

"I'm sad you'll be gone for two years but very happy you're helping with the war effort," Cecil Smith replied.

"We need to impose on you," Nurse Mann interjected.

"This preacher has done more for me than any other living person except maybe my wife Doris. If it's within my power, I'll do it," Cecil Smith responded.

"We want to hire Ruth Bell to move on base with us to be our full-time maid and the twins' nanny," the county nurse admitted.

"Have you talked to her?" Cecil asked.

"We're talking to you first," the preacher said.

"I'm good with that. If it was anyone other than you two, Doris would be as angry as an old wet hen," Cecil Smith said with a chuckle.

"If you'll slip Miss Ruth past Doris, we'll do the asking," Preacher Mann urged.

"My daddy always said that sometimes it's better to ask for forgiveness than ask for permission. I'll motion Miss Ruth to the door and then distract Doris. The rest is up to you," Cecil Smith said as he got up and walked toward the kitchen door of the Bluebird Café.

In just a few minutes, Ruth Bell exited the kitchen door of the Bluebird Café and approached the Manns. She was excited to see the preacher with his wife.

"Lord, I'd never guess it was you two and on a Saturday morning no less," Ruth Bell said with a laugh.

"Miss Ruth, I want you to be our maid and full-time nanny for the twins," Nurse Mann stated.

"I shore enough will, but I've got to give notice to Mr. Cecil and Miss Doris. They've been too good to me for me to just run out on them," Ruth Bell replied.

"Before you fully decide, you need to know the preacher has re-enlisted in the U.S. Army. We're moving to Oak Ridge near Knoxville. I'll be working at the base hospital there. It'll be at least two years before we're back in Ferguson," Nurse Mann explained.

"That don't make me no never mind. I got some kin in Knoxville. That's where Lee and I were going when we first met up with the preacher. That day changed our lives. I'm powerful grateful that the Lord sent him our way," Ruth Bell replied.

"We're really excited about this!" Preacher Mann said excitedly.

Miss Ruth said, "Preacher, I'm just like that old gospel song about Ruth, in the Bible, that the Smith Brothers sing:

**"Whither Thou Go (There I go)**
**Whither Thou Go (There I go)**
**Whither Thou Go (There I go)**
**Thou people shall be my people**
**Thy God, My God (Thy God, My God)**
**Ruth came down (Woman of Moab)**
**Ruth came down (To the land of the Hebrews)**
**Ruth came down (She went on down)**
**To the place that God anointed"**

"We've got thirty days before we have to be on duty at the base. You should work until we leave for

Oak Ridge. Cecil is aware of the situation. It would be best if this were kept quiet. We'll tell you more in the next couple of weeks," Preacher Mann said.

"My mouth is hushed. I'll tell Mr. Cecil that we've made a deal. He can tell Miss Doris," Miss Ruth replied.

Ruth Bell hugged both the preacher and the county nurse. She walked back toward the kitchen door. The Manns stopped at their home. Nurse Mann retrieved the county car to pick up the twins at Miss Rosie's. Preacher Mann stopped at Discount Grocery to summon Josh Sullivan.

"I guess it's a workday. You've got on your preaching clothes," Jack Wright said as the preacher entered Discount Grocery.

"I need you to call The Mountain Gazette and ask Josh to come to see us," the preacher instructed.

"Is it about Nurse Abby? Did her parents call? Are we having a shotgun wedding?" Jack Wright asked in rapid succession.

"It's true. You're totally healed," Preacher Mann opined.

"Did the Lord tell you that? Did Dr. Whitman tell you that?" the merchant asked.

"No, your nosy, gossipy attitude told me that. You're back to normal after a few months lay-off," Preacher Mann opined.

"I'm not gossiping. I'm just asking. I'm a deacon. If something is going on, I've got a right to know about it," Jack Wright said indignantly.

"The scripture says, 'Love thinketh no evil.' Now you have just thought the worst about that young couple. I don't understand why you'd do that," Preacher Mann said chiding the storekeeper.

Before Jack Wright could respond to Preacher Mann's scolding, Josh Sullivan appeared. He was slightly red-faced and out of breath.

"I didn't waste any time. Mr. Wright said it was important," Josh announced.

"Jack, you need to close the store and shut the front door for an early lunch," the preacher instructed.

"Are you buying us lunch at the Bluebird?" the merchant asked.

"I'm going to give you some news that even Louis Barrett doesn't know," the preacher replied.

Jack Wright rushed to the front of the store. He placed a 'Closed For Lunch' sign on the door handle.

When Jack Wright returned and positioned himself beside the counter, the preacher began, "The army higher-ups have written the draft board a confidential letter that Josh Sullivan is to be issued a ministerial exemption from the draft."

"Are you sure the exemption will be granted?" the young preacher answered.

"I am certain of it," Preacher Mann said.

"How can you be so certain?" Jack Wright asked.

"I am certain because the deal included Agent Gary Simpkins and I agreeing to re-enlist, accept commissions as U.S. Army as captains, and serve at the new military base near Knoxville," the preacher explained.

"What are we going to do about a preacher?" Jack Wright inquired.

"Josh Sullivan will be promoted to senior minister in my absence. Otherwise, he won't meet the conditions for the ministerial exemption," Preacher Mann explained.

"I'm good with that. I think the other deacons will be good with that, too," the storekeeper said.

"I need to sit down. I'm getting light-headed. I wasn't expecting this for a few years," the young preacher lamented.

"We're leaving in less than thirty days. You need to get your wedding plans made quickly if you want me to perform the ceremony," Preacher Mann instructed.

"We were hoping to wait a few months until we could get one of those Simpson Meadows homes," Josh said with a stunned look.

"You'll be living in our fully furnished Simpson Meadows house for at least two years. I'll be asking the board of deacons to purchase the home as a minister's residence and make the payment a part of your compensation package," Preacher Mann said.

"I thought we should have been doing that for the past year, but you were against it," Jack Wright said.

"I get a military pension. I get a decent salary for my church work. Beth gets paid for being a senior rural health nurse by the county. We can afford to pay our way," Preacher Mann replied.

"Where's Nurse Mann going to live?" Josh Sullivan asked.

"She'll be living in Oak Ridge with her family. Your soon-to-be bride is getting a promotion, too," the preacher said with a chuckle.

"What do I need to do?" Josh asked.

"Contact the deacons and set a meeting for 6:00 pm tonight at the church. Don't give any details. Blame it on Jack Wright and say it's about the preacher's residence," Preacher Mann instructed.

"Is there anything else?" Josh Sullivan asked.

"Make a date for 7:00 pm tonight with Nurse Abby," the preacher ordered.

"I've actually got a date with her at 7:00 pm at Miss Rosie's," the young man responded.

"Good! Tell her to meet you in Cookeville at 2:00 pm today. Take her to C & C Jewelry and have her pick out a ring. Jack Wright is going with you to make sure you get a good deal," the preacher barked.

"It is tough closing Discount Grocery on a Saturday," Jack Wright said.

"It was tough unloading freight and stocking shelves for Frankie Wright during your convalescence," the preacher replied.

"It can be hard work," the merchant stated.

"It was worse than hearing your wife swoon over all the things she loved about her 'Sweetie,'" Preacher Mann retorted.

"I really liked the one about how he wrapped his toasty warm feet around hers while they laid in bed snuggling and smooching on a cold night," Josh Sullivan remarked.

"Come on, Josh. Let's get to Cookeville and get that ring," Jack Wright insisted.

"Have a safe trip, Sweetie," Preacher Mann said as the trio walked out the front door.

# 14. The Secret City

After a restful day on Monday, following a weekend of announced changes, Preacher Mann and his wife arose early on Tuesday morning to make their way to Clinton Engineering Works in Anderson County. The secret community designated as part of the Manhattan Project would soon become home to the Mann family and their maid and nanny, Ruth Bell.

General Leslie Groves, military head of the Manhattan Project, selected the site for several reasons. Its relatively low population made land acquisition affordable. It was easily accessible by both highway and rail. Utilities such as water and electricity were readily available due to the recent completion of the nearby Norris Dam.

The project location was established within a 17-mile-long valley that was linear and partitioned by several ridges. This provided natural protection against the spread of any disasters resulting from accidents at any of the four industrial plants.

This location, coupled with the relatively low population, helped keep the nuclear town a secret.

The name Oak Ridge was chosen in 1943 from suggestions submitted by project employees.

Nurse Mann asked the preacher to take Highway 27 through Clarkrange, Lancing, and Wartburg to Oak Ridge. It provided a beautiful scenic route transitioning from the Upper Cumberland Plateau to the mountains of east Tennessee. It was roughly the same distance if the county nurse had opted for traveling through Harriman, Tennessee.

"What are your expectations of your meeting with Captain Charles Lowe?" Preacher Mann asked his wife.

"According to Captain John Anderson, medical care will be provided for both army personnel and civilians at a cost of $2.50 per month for individual civilians and five dollars per month for families," Nurse Mann reported.

"What do they expect the potential patient population to grow to become?" the preacher inquired.

"It's about 5,500 people right now," she replied.

"Lawyers call that answer non-responsive," Preacher Mann said.

"I answered your question," Nurse Mann replied.

"My question was about the ultimate patient population," the preacher said pointedly.

"That's classified," his wife responded.